# AMBUSHED!

The security guard directed Frank and Joe into a courtyard surrounded by ivy-covered walls.

"What is this place?" Joe asked.

They both spun around at a loud metallic *boom* behind them. A metal gate had crashed to the ground, sealing off the exit. Then each window in the building was thrown open, and from the second floor up, long ropes flopped to the ground.

"I think we have visitors," Frank said.

Suddenly the walls came alive. Clutching the ropes, a dozen people rappeled downward. Within seconds, they surrounded the brothers. Frank gulped. The black uniforms weren't very welcoming, nor were the flak vests and gas masks.

But the worst—definitely the worst—were the submachine guns, pointed at their heads!

## Books in THE HARDY BOYS CASEFILES™ Series

Available from ARCHWAY Paperbacks

# THE HARDY BOYS CASEFILES NO. 37

# DANGER ZONE

## FRANKLIN W. DIXON

**AN ARCHWAY PAPERBACK**
Published by POCKET BOOKS
New York   London   Toronto   Sydney   Tokyo   Singapore

AN ARCHWAY PAPERBACK *Original*

An Archway Paperback published by
POCKET BOOKS, a division of Simon & Schuster Inc.
1230 Avenue of the Americas, New York, NY 10020

ISBN: 0-671-73751-1

First Archway Paperback Printing March 1990

10  9  8  7  6  5  4  3

# DANGER ZONE

# Chapter

## 1

"BIG HELP YOU ARE. We're going to miss the second half," Joe Hardy grumbled to his brother, pushing a lock of blond hair off his face. He looked down to make sure he'd removed all the glass from a broken soda bottle from around the left rear tire of the Hardys' black van. Then he gripped the handle of a green car jack and pumped. With a series of sudden jerks the van fell back to the parking lot of the supermarket.

"Hey, I offered," Frank replied, standing beside his brother and slowly crumpling an empty potato chip bag. There was a sly glint in his dark brown eyes as he smiled at his younger brother. "I seem to remember someone insisting on doing it himself so we'd get out of here faster." He opened the rear door of the van and tossed the empty bag into a sack of groceries they had just bought.

Joe slipped the jack off, picked up the flat tire along with the jack, and tossed them in the back of the van. They made a loud *thunk* as they hit the floor next to the groceries. "And another thing," he said, retrieving the empty potato chip bag and balling it up. "These were supposed to be for the second half of the game." Joe and Frank's friends were joining them in fifteen minutes for the second half of the NFL game.

To Joe, solving crimes was probably the most important thing in his life. But on a Sunday afternoon in the fall, with the maples blanketing Bayport in a fiery display of color, the pro football game of the week was a close second. Unlike sleuthing, football was simple. There were no terrorists involved, no codes to crack, no bomb threats, no high-speed chases. Just grown men knocking together over a piece of pigskin. Simple. Elegant. At a solidly built six feet, Joe sometimes wondered if he shouldn't try to be a pro player after school.

Frank, an inch taller but leaner than his brother, enjoyed football, too. He wasn't in love with the game itself—it was okay—but he was in love with the way the games worked his brother into a frenzy. Their detective father,

Fenton Hardy, who was away on some myste-rious "security gig in southwestern Massachu-setts," was the major calming influence on Joe. Without him it promised to be a better show than usual, Frank decided.

"Joe, there are four more bags in there—family size. Not to mention the pretzels, the popcorn, the burgs, the dogs, the kielbasa, and the ice cream. I think we'll survive for two quarters of a game."

Glowering, Joe stepped around to the driv-er's door and climbed in.

Frank leaned in through the passenger win-dow. "But it you're really worried about it, I can always go back in and—"

"Very funny, Frank," Joe said. "Come on, let's get out of here. I don't want to be slaving over a hot barbecue when the game's on." As Frank got in he put the key in the ignition and gunned the engine.

Frank nodded. "I can just see it now. The quarterback sweeps around the line for a ninety-eight-yard end run. The crowd is on its feet, screaming. Biff Hooper is so excited he crushes his soda can, sending a geyser of grape soda all over Phil Cohen's new T-shirt. Chet Morton stops feeding his face for a record three full seconds and bursts into hysterics. And where's Joe Hardy during all this action? Outside by the grill, helping Aunt Gertrude arrange hot dog buns around the kielbasa.''

The only answer to Frank's scenario was a squeal of tires as the van tore out of the parking lot.

Frank gripped the door handle. "Whoa, ease up! We run over one more soda bottle, and we're walking! That was our only spare."

Joe slowed down as he scanned the asphalt parking lot. "I still say that bottle wasn't there when I pulled in. I would have felt it."

"Maybe some kids smashed the bottle when we were inside."

"Nope. That wouldn't explain how the tire blew unless the kids slashed the tire. Maybe those new shock absorbers Dad put in are doing one unbelievable job, and we just didn't feel it."

Joe turned left out of the lot and drove through the familiar suburban streets of Bayport, taking a strategic route that avoided all the traffic lights. Within minutes they were pulling into the gravel driveway of a large, handsome stone house.

Joe leaned on the horn. "We're home, Mom and Aunt Gertrude! Fire up that grill!"

Frank and Joe climbed out and ran around the back of the van. They yanked the door open, pulled out the four grocery bags, and carried them across the front to the walkway.

Suddenly Frank stopped in front of Joe, almost causing him to drop his bags. "Hey, what are you . . ."

Joe's question trailed off when he saw what Frank was staring at.

The inner front door was wide open. On a warm late-September afternoon, that wasn't unusual.

It was the storm door that caught Frank's attention. It was open, too.

"What—" Frank muttered under his breath, sensing that something was wrong.

The brothers dropped their bags and raced inside. A bottle of ketchup cracked dully on the path behind them.

They stopped short in the living room. Beside the fireplace a marble coffee table lay on its side. Next to it lay the shattered pieces of a glass paperweight.

"Mom! Aunt Gertrude!" Joe called into the house. He and Frank bolted into the dining room, then the kitchen. There the table had been pushed against a wall, toppling two of the chairs.

"Oh, no." Frank's voice caught in his throat. He was staring at the cutlery drawer by the refrigerator—or, rather, the open space where the drawer had been. On the floor was a gleaming mass of silverware spilled out on the floor.

Joe ran to the back door. It was open. He went outside, calling his mom's name. The deck furniture, the garage, the lawn—everything back there was in place.

Meanwhile Frank checked the den and Mr. Hardy's office. Nothing was suspiciously out of place there. Next he bounded upstairs. Joe's bedroom looked ransacked, but that was normal. In the other bedrooms Frank saw no signs of a struggle, but there were no signs of his mother or aunt, either.

The brothers arrived back in the kitchen at the same time. Joe's brow was creased. His eyes darted from object to object, following the inner rhythm of his thoughts. "Frank, we've got to figure this out," he said, pacing the floor. "Who would do this? What if something has happened to them?"

Joe's last question was an anguished shout.

Frank gripped Joe firmly by the arm. "We can't let our emotions take over, Joe. We owe it to Mom and Aunt Gertrude to treat this professionally."

The words were coming out, but they didn't sound convincing. Joe looked into his brother's eyes and saw the same fear that was in his. But somehow it made Frank's thoughts slow down and focus.

"Okay. If Mom was attacked, she'd know

enough to leave a trace of something. Wouldn't she?''

Joe didn't like the tone of doubt in Frank's voice. "Right," he said. "Right." He knelt beside the spilled silverware, looking for something—anything.

Frank turned toward the dining room. He took a step into the room and stopped cold.

"Frank, what if—"

"Ssh!"

Joe let the question fall off. He froze, listening for whatever Frank had heard.

In the silence, it came. A barely audible bumping noise. Once . . . twice . . . the third time it was accompanied by a muffled crack.

"The den closet!" Frank shouted. The brothers sprang into action. They sped past the stairs and into the den. Joe got to the closet first and yanked it open.

A cloth bag five and a half feet high toppled toward him. It was obvious that inside the bag was a human form.

"Mom!" Joe yelled, and he caught her in his arms. He dragged the bag to the sofa and untied a knot at the top. Frank immediately pulled the bag down.

Bound with a heavy rope, her hair matted with perspiration and her mouth gagged, was Aunt Gertrude!

Frank pulled off the gag as Joe struggled to untie her.

"Oh!" Aunt Gertrude cried out. "Oh!"

"Are you all right?" Frank asked.

Aunt Gertrude nodded weakly as Frank picked her up and set her gently on the sofa. "I—I think so," she gasped. "It—it was so awful—that man—that terrible, evil—I tried to—I couldn't—"

Joe removed the last of the binding. "It's all right, Aunt Gertrude. Everything's all right."

"Oh, thank you, boys. I tried to knock, but my hands were tied. All I could do was bump my body against the door. I thought you'd never hear me!"

"We're here, Aunt Gertrude," Frank reassured her. "It's all over. Can you tell us what happened? Where's Mom?"

"I—I tried to get a knife from the drawer," Aunt Gertrude barreled on, "but one of them— one of them just pulled the whole drawer out!"

"One of whom, Aunt Gertrude?" Frank asked.

"I don't know! They were wearing masks. Terrible black masks! Ohhh—how could those beasts have done that to her—"

Aunt Gertrude's eyes started to well with tears. Frank and Joe exchanged a terrified glance.

"Aunt Gertrude," Frank said softly, "where's Mom?"

A rapid set of snuffles was all the answer Aunt Gertrude could give. Her trembling right hand reached up to her heart, and she closed her eyes.

When she opened them they were shot through with cold, naked fear.

"Boys, your mother—" Aunt Gertrude's lips began quivering, and Frank was afraid she wouldn't finish her sentence.

But she did.

"Your mother has been kidnapped!"

# Chapter

## 2

"ARE YOU SURE, Aunt Gertrude?" Joe said urgently. "Did you see them?"

Aunt Gertrude nodded. "Yes, yes. Of course I'm sure. Oh, the poor dear. There was nothing I could do." She shook her head, fighting back tears, starting to get angry now. "You boys—I always *told* you this detective nonsense would amount to no good! Look at what's happened."

"Please, Aunt Gertrude," Frank said softly, "describe what happened. You were in the house when—"

"I was not in the house," Aunt Gertrude contradicted him. "I was out taking a walk. It seemed so splendid outside, and the old maple tree by the Remsens' house is one of the first to turn, so I figured I'd go there to check it out and chat a bit. I brought them some jam—''

"And you came back," Joe pressed on impatiently.

"Yes. I came back and noticed both front doors open. Well, of course, I thought, That's not like Laura to leave the doors open, even on a beautiful day. You know flies and mosquitoes are still thriving. . . .''

Frank realized that Aunt Gertrude couldn't have been hurt too much. She was rambling on like her old self. Frank felt himself getting as impatient as his brother.

"Then I repeated to myself, Laura just wouldn't leave *both* doors open like that!" Aunt Gertrude continued. "So I went inside, and the first thing I saw was the mess in the living room. Well, I was shocked. Then I heard noises inside—rough male voices. I called out, 'Laura?' and walked to the kitchen. And that's when I—saw her.'' Aunt Gertrude shuddered. A small sob escaped, and her eyes began to mist over.

"What happened?" Joe demanded, his eyes on fire. "Was she—"

"Alive?" Aunt Gertrude cut in. "Yes. At least I think she was. She—" Suddenly she began sobbing violently, and tears started to flow down her cheeks. "To tell the truth, boys, I don't even know for sure! She was on the

11

floor, and they were—oh, it was so barbaric!— they were stuffing her into a sack like that one!" She pointed to the bag that had been covering her.

Frank handed her a tissue from a nearby box. "How many of them?" he pressed.

Aunt Gertrude's fingers fluttered nervously as she dabbed her cheeks. "Two. Yes, there were two men holding the bag. They both looked up as I walked in. I screamed—oh, I thought I'd lose my voice—"

"And then they turned on you," Joe interjected.

"Well, no, they didn't. They were both just staring at me when that horrible old bag was pulled over my head."

"So there had to be at least *three* of them," Joe interrupted. "One to pull the bag over your head."

"Yes, I suppose there were three."

"What did they look like?" Frank asked.

"I—I couldn't tell. . . ." She looked away as her thoughts wandered back. "The blond one was wearing a ski mask—"

"Blond one?" Joe repeated. "How could you tell his hair color if he wore a ski mask?"

"It was tucked up in back, and I saw a blond fringe," Aunt Gertrude answered.

"Did you notice anything else about him?" Frank asked.

Her eyes lit up. "Come to think of it, I did notice something else. Yes—in fact, I know who he was!"

Frank gave her a strong, encouraging smile. "Way to go, Aunt Gertrude! Who?"

Aunt Gertrude looked at her nephews with renewed confidence. She set her chin triumphantly and said, "A forest ranger."

Frank's face fell. He could see his brother's shoulders slump. "A *what?*"

"Am I not enunciating clearly, or do you both have cotton in your ears? A forest ranger! Yes, that must be who it was. I *knew* I'd seen one of those shirts before. It was exactly like the shirts those rangers wore on my trip to Yellowstone National Park—oh, about ten or twelve years ago, do you remember? Probably not—you were so young at the time. Back then I had hoped that you boys might become rangers. But will you listen to me ramble on and on? You'd think I was an old lady."

"It's just the shock. Shock makes us all act differently," Frank said, trying to soothe his aunt.

Joe gave his brother an exasperated look. Shaking his head, he stood up and walked to the other end of the room.

A forest ranger in a coastal town like Bayport, New York, could be a lead. But Gertrude could have been wrong about the shirt, or the

13

guy could have bought the shirt at a second-hand shop.

Aunt Gertrude finally fell silent, then began to rise. "Well, I can't look for your mother, but I can pick up. That kitchen is such a terrible mess." As she stood her legs buckled beneath her.

Frank reached out and grabbed her hand. "Please, Aunt Gertrude, just try to rest. Besides, it's best to leave everything the way it is. The police will want to search for clues." He got up and turned to Joe. "I'll be right back."

Frank went into the kitchen so his aunt could rest and stepped over a fallen chair to get to the phone.

As soon as he reached for it, it rang.

He snatched it off the hook. "Hello, who is this?"

There was a brief pause. "Well, aren't you being a little presumptuous? You haven't yet told me who *you* are."

The voice sent a chill up Frank's spine. It sounded as if it were being programmed letter by letter through a computer voice sampler.

No, that couldn't be, Frank immediately realized. The voice had answered his question, so it couldn't have been recorded in advance.

"This is Frank Hardy. Now get to the point, pal. I need to use this phone."

14

"We are dispensing with the formalities, are we, Frank Hardy?" the voice replied. "I can go along with that."

A scrambler. That's what he was using, Frank realized. An electronic device held up to the receiver that disguises the voice by filtering it through different frequencies.

Frank moved toward the den. Behind him the extra-long telephone extension cord was stretched taut. He could just see his brother sitting on the couch next to Aunt Gertrude.

"In fact, perhaps I can alleviate your sense of urgency," the eerie voice went on. "You see, you will not be needing to use the phone after our conversation."

Frantically Frank signaled to Joe by waving a hand over his head.

"Yeah?" he said, stalling for time. "I think I'm the one who'll decide that!"

Joe looked up. Gesturing, Frank mouthed the words *the phone in Dad's den*. Joe immediately stood up. Frank then twisted his arm as if turning a knob and mouthed *tape recorder*.

Joe bolted from the room.

"Have it your way," the voice replied. Through the odd, disjointed tone Frank could hear an undercurrent of threat. "I would be terribly disappointed if you didn't do what I suggest. It would be a shame to see a noble woman like Mrs. Hardy suffer because of her son's stubbornness.''

Frank froze. In the silence he heard an almost imperceptible click as Joe picked up Fenton's phone.

"What did you do with my mother?" Frank asked through clenched teeth.

"Your mother, I'm pleased to say, is enjoying quite pleasant accommodations. And you *do* want to keep it that way, don't you?"

Hoping that Joe was recording the conversation, Frank said, "All right, let's cut the phony politeness. You'll be dead meat if my mom is hurt, buddy, so you might as well tell me what's going down right now."

"Dead meat," the voice repeated. "A colorful but rather repulsive image, don't you think? What's going down, my hotheaded young friend, is simply this: Fenton Hardy must be back at your house in twenty-four hours to answer a phone call. In person. Is that clear?"

Instinctively Frank looked at his watch, which read five-thirty. "And what if he's not?"

"Must you ask so many questions?" the voice answered. It chuckled malevolently, making a sound not unlike broken glass scratching a blackboard. "If he's not, your beloved mother will die."

# Chapter

## 3

THERE WAS A HOLLOW CLICK at the other end of the phone. Frank stared at it unseeing for a few seconds before he hung up.

Joe appeared in the hallway outside the den. He looked over his shoulder to check on Gertrude, then walked toward Frank. "That slimeball," he hissed. "If he laid a finger on Mom—"

"Did you get the voice on tape?" Frank interrupted, his face taut with concentration.

"Yeah, but a lot of good that's going to do us. The guy was using a scrambler, so we can't run a voice-pattern test. There's no way we can involve the police after what he said."

"We're just going to have to find Dad. Obviously this guy doesn't want to talk to us."

"Great," Joe retorted. "Only Mom knows

where he is. What do we do, call information for the state of Massachusetts and say, 'Fenton Hardy, please. He's on a secret intelligence trip somewhere in the southwestern part of your state. Can you locate him?' Frank, this guy's got us over a barrel.''

"I'm not so sure," Frank said. He cast a concerned glance toward the den. "Let's get Aunt Gertrude upstairs. Then I want to hear that tape again."

They went into the den to find Aunt Gertrude still sitting on the couch, her head back, her eyes shut. "No . . . no," she mumbled. "Leave my sister-in-law alone. She has two youngsters. If you must take someone, take me!"

Joe raised an eyebrow. "Youngsters?" he repeated under his breath.

Frank reached out and gently folded his hand over his aunt's. "Come on. I think you need a rest, Aunt Gertrude."

Her eyes fluttered open. "Frank! My goodness, did I fall asleep?"

Frank nodded.

"Who was on the phone?" she asked with sudden hope. "Was it Fenton?"

"No," Joe replied, thinking fast. "It was—uh—an electronic voice. You know, one of those tape recordings that tries to sell you things."

Aunt Gertrude nodded absently. "And for

that the two of you had to rush off, leaving me all alone?'' Joe opened his mouth to answer, but she waved him off. ''Never mind. I suppose I can't expect you to act normally when your dear mother has been—'' Her voice choked in the middle of the sentence.

''Please, Aunt Gertrude,'' Frank said, urging her toward the stairs. ''We'll get in touch with Dad. Why don't you have a little nap? I'm sure you'll feel better.''

Protesting feebly, she allowed her nephews to take her up to her room. They sat her down on her bed, and before they were out of the room she had curled up and fallen asleep.

They quietly skittered down the stairs, walked into their father's office, and sat down.

''Now we know for sure we didn't run over that soda bottle in the parking lot. The kidnappers punctured the tire to keep us occupied while they took Mom,'' Joe said.

''You're right,'' Frank agreed. ''I think we should study the tape, listen to this guy's accent, listen for background noise. Did you set the ticker when you turned it on?''

''What do you think I am, an amateur?'' Joe rewound to *000* and played the tape back:

''Your mother, I'm pleased to say, is enjoying quite pleasant accommodations. . . .''

It was impossible to detect an accent, Frank

thought. The voice was so garbled it could have come from Mars. But there was another sound.

"And you do want to—"

"Stop there!" Frank said.

Joe already had. There had been two high-pitched squeals in the background. He re-wound and played again. They listened closely to the squeals.

"They sound like screams!" Joe said.

Frank shook his head. "My guess is the scraping of a table leg against the floor, or some feedback into the mike."

"Or a dog barking, or an elephant bleating, or the squeak of grease as this nut twirls his handlebar mustache." Joe slumped into the brown leather chair by his father's desk. "It could be anything! That scrambler is mixing up any noise that comes through the mike."

Something was dawning on Frank, but he couldn't tell Joe. Not just yet. "I guess we're going to have to do what the man says, Joe," he said in a loud voice.

Joe looked at him as if he'd just lost his mind. "But we don't know—"

"We'll find him. I've got to go check the secret phone file."

"Secret phone—"

Joe's answer was interrupted by the loud tramping of footsteps on the living room floor.

"Hey! What's going on?" a voice boomed.

Frank ran out of the room, leaving a bewildered Joe to follow him. "Chet!" he called.

When he got to the living room Chet Morton was standing there, dumbfounded. His broad shoulders had gone slack, making his potbelly jut out even more than usual. Drooping from his left hand was a half-eaten slice of pizza. "What did you guys do to this place?"

Behind him Phil Cohen was squeezing his thin body behind an armchair to unplug a lamp whose bulb had shattered. Biff Hooper was standing on the opposite side of the room from Chet. Together they looked like two useless pillars of a building that had collapsed around them.

"I wish," Frank said with a rueful smile. He quickly told them what had happened. They listened with a mixture of dread, disbelief, and anger.

"We'll trace the call!" Chet said, jutting his pizza forward to emphasize his point. "My dad knows a guy who works for the phone company—"

"Phil," Frank said, cutting Chet off, "can I talk to you out in the backyard?"

Tilting his head quizzically, Phil said, "Sure."

Frank turned to his brother. "Joe, you and the guys straighten up. We'll be right back."

Frank moved through the house with Phil

close behind. Together they stepped into the backyard.

"What's this all about?" Phil asked.

"I need your expertise," Frank replied. "About electronics."

He pulled open the garage door and reached around to flick on the light. Mrs. Hardy's car stood on the left side, dwarfed by the shelves that reached upward all around it. Each shelf was stuffed with boxes and boxes of tools, gadgets, and equipment. Frank reached into an unmarked metal box on a bottom shelf.

"I can't believe you can find anything in this mess," Phil commented, shaking his head.

"Actually, it's very easy," Frank replied. "The trick is living in this house for eighteen years." He pulled out a long, sturdy metal loop with a rubber handle and a small white gauge.

Phil asked, "What are you going to do with an inductance coil?"

"Can it detect a current hidden behind a hard surface, like a wall?"

Phil shrugged. "Sure. It's a closed electric circuit with no juice of its own. But if you hold it near an electric circuit, it picks up current, and the meter jumps. What do you need it for, Frank?"

"Follow me," Frank answered.

He ran back to the house. Holding the coil,

Phil followed him to the living room. There, Joe, Chet, and Biff were setting up furniture.

"What's going on?" Joe asked.

"No clues back there," Frank answered.

"I could have told you that," Joe said, giving Frank a bewildered look.

But Frank was walking away from him toward a small table by the couch. On the table was a message pad, a pen, and a telephone. Wordlessly, Frank looked at Phil and pointed to the wall behind the table.

Phil nodded knowingly and began to run the inductance coil along the wall.

Before anyone could ask any questions Frank said, "The place looks much better. Let's get started on the kitchen."

Realizing that something was up, Joe led the others into the kitchen. Frank stayed behind and watched as Phil passed the coil along the wall behind the phone table . . . the couch . . . the armchair. . . .

Suddenly the needle on the meter jumped, then settled back. Phil's eyes lit up. He began to say something, but Frank held out his hand, signaling him to be quiet.

Phil slowly brought the coil back. When the needle jumped again Phil held it at the spot. He turned to Frank with a triumphant smile.

Frank nodded, then immediately indicated Phil to follow him again. The two of them went into the kitchen, where Frank waved everyone outside. "Let's put the barbecue grill away, guys, okay?"

"Barbe—" Chet began, but Frank grabbed him by the arm and pulled him out the back door.

One by one, with mystified looks on their faces, they stepped out into the backyard. Frank led them to a secluded spot under an oak tree.

"Okay, what's all the cloak-and-dagger stuff?" Chet demanded. "Don't tell me there's a bomb hidden inside or something."

"Not a bomb, Chet," Frank replied. "A bug. Whoever this kidnapper is, he was listening to every word we said in the house!"

# Chapter

## 4

"YOU MEAN WE WERE ON 'Candid Microphone'?" Chet remarked. "If I'd known, I would have *really* said what was on my mind!"

"I just hope we didn't let out anything important," Phil said.

Joe shook his head. "What's there to hide? We don't know where Dad is. Maybe they'll believe us."

"That's weird," Phil said.

"What's weird?" Joe replied.

"Your dad just left town without telling you where he was going?" Phil asked.

"'Southwestern Massachusetts' was all he said," Frank replied with a shrug. "That's the way it goes—sometimes he has to keep things secret."

25

"I can't believe he wouldn't leave a number," Chet said.

"My mom knows," Frank replied.

"Doesn't do you and Joe a whole lot of good," Biff said. "It's not like you can call her and ask."

Joe furrowed his brow. "No, but I do remember them talking about my dad's assignment a week or so ago. They were upstairs, and I was passing their room. I could hear them."

All eyes focused on Joe. "What did they say?" Frank asked.

"The usual stuff," Joe said, running the hazy events over in his mind. "Mom sounded a little annoyed. She asked if he had to go. Dad said unfortunately yes. Mom mentioned how much work there was to do around the house, Dad said he'd do most of it before he left. Mom asked if he'd call her once he got to . . ." His voice trailed off.

"To where, Joe?" Frank pressed.

Joe put his hand to his forehead. "I wasn't really paying attention! I wanted to get back to my room. Now, let's see. What was the name of that town? *Mar* something."

"Marbury," Phil suggested.

"Marshalltown," Biff said.

"Marmalade!" Chet blurted out.

Biff rolled his eyes. "You marshmallow," he muttered.

Frank ran into the house to get a New England map as the others continued to suggest names. Scurrying back outside, he opened to a list of towns at the bottom of the map.

"Marfield," he called out, reading from the Massachusetts section of the list. "Marion, Marlborough, Marstons Mills—"

"Wait!" Joe interrupted. "Marfield—that rings a bell. I think that was it. 'Fenton, will you call me as soon as you get to Marfield?' I'm not positive, but I'm pretty sure that's what she said!"

"That's as good a lead as any," Frank responded.

"And Dad told her he couldn't call—he had to remain strictly incommunicado. That much I do remember clearly!"

Frank looked levelly at Phil. "Joe and I are out of here. Can you destroy the bug? I don't care what you do to the wall."

"You got it," Phil answered, running inside.

"Great. The rest of you guys stick around, guard the house, make sure Aunt Gertrude is all right. We'll call from the road and give you a progress report."

While he was speaking Frank looked from Phil to Biff to Chet. Only Chet's face reflected the doubt they were all feeling.

27

"The fridge is full. Help yourselves," Frank added. All three of them nodded their agreement.

Frank and Joe ran inside and up to their rooms. They each threw some changes of clothing and a toothbrush into a duffel bag, checked to see that their aunt was still asleep, then headed back downstairs. As they barreled toward the back door Phil's voice called out from behind them, "Wait a sec! Take this. You may need it."

Frank turned around to see Phil holding the inductance coil out to him. "What about the other rooms in the house?"

"I checked the kitchen, the dining room, and your dad's office," Phil answered. "I did it quickly, but I'm pretty sure they're all clean. Biff found a hole hidden behind the living room couch, which is how they got the bug in. Obviously these guys didn't have time to cover their tracks; I have a feeling they only planted the one bug."

"Okay," Frank said, taking the coil. Calling out a hurried goodbye, he and Joe climbed into the van and took off.

Frank stopped briefly at the end of the driveway before pulling into the street. Instinctively he and Joe cased both sides of the street. There were four parked cars.

"Do you see any drivers?" Frank said.

"Nope, they all look empty to me," Joe said.

"We'll see about that." Frank stepped on the gas and took a left. He trained his eye on the rearview mirror, but none of the parked cars followed them.

"Looks like we're alone," Joe said, glancing up and down the quiet intersections they passed. "But just in case, let's take the scenic route."

"Aye, aye, captain," Frank replied, taking a sudden right turn. As he wound quickly through the streets of Bayport Joe hung on to his armrest.

Ten minutes later Frank finally pulled onto a road that would lead them to the expressway.

"There," he said. "If anyone could follow *that,* I'll burn my driver's license."

Joe looked behind them. About thirty yards back was a dark blue Buick. "You'll burn it, huh? I wonder if there are any matches in the glove compartment."

"What?"

"Maybe I'm being paranoid, but check out the rearview mirror."

Frank glanced up just as Joe spotted an abandoned gas station ahead of them. In the center island were two covered-up holes with dusty wires and hoses sticking out.

"Slow down," Joe suggested. He pointed to the entrance. "Turn in there."

Frank stepped on the brake, then turned. Gravel bounced on the cracked and broken concrete as the car rolled in.

Behind them the Buick quietly pulled over to the shoulder and waited.

"If there aren't any matches, I guess we could use the cigarette lighter on your license," Joe commented.

Without saying a word Frank floored the gas pedal and tore out onto the street. Tires screeched behind them as the Buick pursued.

"I don't know how this guy found us," Frank said, "but his luck is about to run out."

He took a sharp left onto a deserted road that ran past a cornfield. The Buick followed. Frank floored the gas pedal, putting distance between them and their pursuers. As the road curved to the left he momentarily lost sight of the car in his mirror.

Up ahead was a fork. Frank went right, then immediately turned right again onto a side street. He barreled down this road, then went left at a light that turned red just after he went through. A commercial area lay ahead, with shops lining either side of the street. Beyond it five roads fed into a traffic circle. Frank chose one of them, which trailed off into a residential area.

Keeping his eyes trained on the empty road

behind them, Joe let out a whoop of excitement. "No *way* that guy can find us now!"

"Check the map," Frank said. "They're going to expect us to take the main expressway. Find us a different route."

A cry of disgust from Joe cut Frank off. "I don't believe it!"

Frank looked up and caught a glimpse of the Buick in his rearview mirror. "How did he—"

Before he could finish Joe reached for the glove compartment. Yanking it open, he pulled out a pen and an old white envelope. In seconds he had scribbled a note and handed it to his brother. Frank held it up so that he could read it without taking his eyes off the road: "We're being bugged! The coil's going nuts."

Frank stole a quick look at his brother, who began rolling his arms as if to say *keep talking*.

"This guy's going to follow us all the way to North Carolina!" Frank said. Joe gave him an okay sign as he crawled into the rear of the van. "But I think I know a way to lose him. We'll take Kirkland Road and shoot into one of those dirt paths near the academy. I think I can get us back to the highway from there."

Joe plopped down into the passenger seat, holding a small electronic box with wires dangling from it. "Got it!" he said.

In the rearview mirror Frank saw the Buick

suddenly speed up. He swerved onto a sandy side road that cut between two marshes.

"You know what I think?" Joe said. "This thing isn't a bug, it's a homing device! That would explain how he's been able to tail us so perfectly."

"Well, there's only one way to find out for sure," Frank said. "Let's ask him. It's time we confronted this guy, Joe."

With that, he stepped on the brake and forced the van into a ninety- degree skid. When it stopped it was blocking the road broadside.

"Let's get this guy, Joe," Frank said.

As Frank reached for his door handle he heard the Buick's tires squealing. He looked up to see the car careening toward them and then coming to a sudden, lurching stop. The sun, beginning to set in the western sky, glinted off a shiny metal object in the passenger window of the Buick.

"Duck!" Frank shouted.

Before the word left his mouth the van windows were being shattered with a barrage of machine-gun fire!

# Chapter
## 5

FRANK DROPPED to the van floor, protecting his head with his arms. Above him shards of glass were being spit into the van. There was a sickening *tuck-a-tuck-a-tuck* of metal against metal as bullets raked the sides of the van. The guy with the machine gun didn't know it, but he would never penetrate the interior of the van. The sides were lined with thick sheets of metal.

Like a trapped animal Frank hunkered as low as he could with the pedals in the way and waited for the attack to be over. For a moment he forgot about Joe, forgot about their mission, forgot about everything except the possibility that the attacker would move in and shoot them.

When the attack finally stopped Frank was first aware of the immense silence. Then he noticed that his jaw ached from gritting his teeth, that his brother was alive beside him, and that the Buick was making a getaway.

He rose cautiously and peered out the driver's window. Its tires spinning on the sandy road, the Buick was in the middle of a U-turn. Frank stared, focusing on the small rectangular plate between the two taillights.

As it sped away Joe scrambled up from a crouch and joined Frank. "Did we make it," he asked, "or is this the big van in the sky?"

"We were lucky, Joe," Frank said. "They didn't aim for the tires."

"Yeah, that's because they were aiming higher—at us!" Joe replied. "We'd better check out the engine." Frank turned the key as Joe popped the hood. "Looks and sounds okay. We were really lucky. By the way, did you get the license number?"

"You bet." Frank reached for the dashboard and grabbed the note that Joe had given him. "Where's that pen you were using?"

Joe uncurled his fist to reveal a cracked ballpoint pen and his fingers smeared with dark blue ink. "Uh, right here."

A smile curled up on Frank's lips. "You weren't *too* nervous there, were you?"

"Cool as a cucumber," Joe remarked, holding out the pen. "Nothing more relaxing than a little late-afternoon strafing."

Frank took a rag from the back of the van, wiped off the pen, and wrote down *NZE-809*. "It was a Massachusetts plate."

"The plot thickens," Joe said. He rubbed his fingers with the rag, trying to wipe off the blue stain. "Unfortunately, so does this ink."

"There's got to be a way to find out whose plate that is." Frank tapped the pen agitatedly on the steering wheel. "Too bad we don't know any Massachusetts cops. They could give us access to the Motor Vehicle Department computer list."

"Well, we're near Chartwell Academy. Maybe there are some genius hackers there still." Joe smiled slyly, remembering how he and Frank had broken a criminal computer ring at the school.

Frank's face brightened. "That's it, Joe!"

"Hey, I was joking. We don't know anybody there. They've all been expelled—"

"Right. But we do know a pretty amazing hacker, and he happens to live in Cambridge, Massachusetts!"

"The Beast!" Joe exclaimed. "Of course!"

"Larry Biester, the pride of the Harvard computer science department," Frank said, grabbing the mobile phone. "He helped us crack an international spy ring, and I think he just might be able to help us with the DMV."

Quickly he dialed the Beast's number from memory. The phone rang twice.

"Hello," Larry's voice said. "I'm not in right now, but if you leave your name . . ."

Frank exhaled with disappointment. "He's out."

". . . number and time of day you called, I'll get back to you. Just wait for the beep."

After a faint beep tone Frank said, "Hi, Larry, this is Frank Hardy. It's seven-thirty on Sunday. Call me back right away at—"

"Oh, hi, Frank," Larry's voice interrupted. Frank frowned. "Larry?"

"Yeah, it's me, live. Sounded like a real machine, huh? I'm trying to keep the administration off my tail for a couple of days. They're after me for some money."

"Oh," Frank said. "Listen, Larry, we need your help. I know it's a long shot, but do you think you can break the computer code on the Massachusetts Department of Motor Vehicles? I want to find out who owns a car with plate number—"

"Whoa, whoa! Stop right there!" Larry said. "I'm in enough trouble as it is. If any one of the university bigwigs finds out I've been— uh—free-lancing with the state government, I may be taking a semester off."

"It's important, Larry."

"Yeah? So's my diploma, at least to my parents."

"This has to do with *my* parents," Frank pressed on. "My mother, to be exact. Someone's kidnapped her. Whoever it is is trying to get my father, too—and they just came after us with a machine gun!"

There was stunned silence on the other side. "Whoa. When do you want the info—yesterday? You got it. Just give me two numbers—the license and your phone."

Frank passed on the numbers, thanked him, and said goodbye.

The illuminated digital clock on the dashboard read 12:33 A.M. as Frank exited off onto Marfield Road from the highway. It seemed as though the rest of the world had folded up for the night. The chirping of birds had long since faded away, and all he could hear was the monotonous trill of crickets and the engine's quiet hum. He felt as though he'd be lulled to sleep if it weren't for the cold night air that washed in over him from the shot-out driver's window. Beside him Joe had already fallen victim, bundled up in his jacket. His head lolled lazily to the left against the headrest, and his body bounced slightly with every dip in the road.

Joe had promised not to fall asleep during the five-hour trip, and Frank fought the urge to whack him on the shoulder as a reminder. But he knew that at least *one* of them should get some rest, so he left his brother alone. Besides, they were bound to reach a motel eventually.

"Eventually" turned out to be about ten minutes. As Frank drove along a sleepy section of Marfield Road a neon sign flashed "Marfield Motor Hotel" in the distance. He blinked twice to make sure it wasn't a mirage, then slowed down.

" 'Vacancy,' " he muttered, reading the sign's bottom line.

There was a grunt from Joe's side of the van, then a muffled, slurred voice: "Don't worry. I've got my eyes on the exit signs."

"Well, no need to work so hard anymore," Frank replied. "We're here."

"Huh?" Joe sat up. "Marfield Motor Hotel? How did we—did I fall asleep?"

Frank pulled into the motel's driveway. "Halfway through Connecticut," Frank answered. "But it's okay. I've been enjoying the scenery and the nice, brisk windstorm."

"Arggh!" Joe arched his back as he stretched. "I feel like I've been in a trash compactor."

"I'm sure this place will feel like the Taj Mahal by comparison," Frank remarked. He parked the van far from the entrance so the owner wouldn't see the condition of the van. It could be hard to explain why they were riding in a car riddled with bullet holes.

Joe staggered out of the other side and looked around. The parking lot was nearly empty, and the windows of the squat white building stared blankly at them. Every few seconds, when the neon light flashed, the motel glowed purple.

"I'm not so sure about this place," Joe said. "You know, the back of the van isn't that uncomfortable."

"Come on," Frank insisted. "We won't get too far tomorrow if we don't get some sleep." He walked toward the door to the motel office. Above it hung a smaller sign. This one said "Open 24 Hours".

On the road behind them a lone car whizzed by in the dark.

Frank pulled open the screen door and walked into a small, empty room. A dozen or so keys hung from a pegboard behind a long, wood-paneled counter. On top of the counter was a metal bell with a button on top and a squeaking metal fan that blew a weak stream of air.

"Hello," Frank called out, slapping the button. A loud *ding* pierced the air.

"Yeeaahhh!" came a sudden scream from behind the counter.

"Down, Frank!" Joe shouted.

An unexpected bolt of fear shot through Frank. The two brothers ducked.

Above them a meek voice said, "What's going on? Is anybody there?"

Frank and Joe stood up. Peering over the counter was a short, slender man with wispy hair combed to cover a bald spot. "Uh, sorry about that," Joe said sheepishly. "You scared us. You see, we're kind of tired—"

"Well, that makes three of us," the man said crossly. "Do you boys realize it's almost one in the morning?"

Frank pointed toward the door. "But your sign says twenty-four—"

"Never mind," the man interrupted, pulling out a frayed, vinyl-covered ledger book. "Do you have a reservation?"

"No," Joe answered, "but it doesn't seem like we need—"

"You know, you're lucky. This is the only place in town that has any vacancies tonight." He opened the book and placed a pen inside it. "Sign here."

As Joe picked up the pen the man narrowed his eyes at him. "Say, you're not the fella who called a couple hours ago asking about vacancies, are you?"

"Nope," Joe said, signing two aliases, Peter and Jules Mansfield, just in case.

"All right," the man replied doubtfully, taking a key off the pegboard behind him and throwing it on the counter. "You're in room J. Checkout time is ten. Pay me when you return the key."

"Thank you," Frank said. As the two of them left Joe pointed to the mat in front of the door. The words Courtesy Is Contagious stared up at them.

"I guess the disease has been cured around here," Joe remarked.

Frank peered in the window to see the man disappearing behind the counter again. He followed Joe to room J, which was directly behind the large neon sign. When they shut the door, the room glowed a hideous shade of purple and then darkened as the sign did. Frank flicked on the light to reveal a square room with beige cinder-block walls, two beds, and a table with a phone.

"Taj Mahal, huh?" Joe said, his face suddenly purple. "I'm not so tired."

"Good," Frank replied, opening a drawer in the phone table. "Then you can help me figure out where we're going to look for Dad tomorrow."

He pulled out a phone book and dropped it on the bed. It hardly bounced. "I can see it's

41

going to be a comfortable night," Joe mumbled.

Frank and Joe riffled through the phone book. It wasn't hard to find potential places; most of the industry in the area was centered around a few big technological companies. Before long Frank had compiled a short list of names and addresses on a sheet of Marfield Motor Hotel stationery.

"Foreman Aerospace . . . the Center for Experimental Research . . . Prometheus Computing," Frank said, reading the list. "I think that'll be a good start."

"Anything to get us out of here," Joe yawned. "I don't know about you, but I'm ready for some shut-eye, even if my dreams end up looking purple."

Frank put away the phone book and lay down on one of the beds. "See you in the morning."

"Yeah," Joe replied, flopping down on his bed. And as his head hit the pillow he was asleep.

*Brriing!*

As Monday's early light broke through the windows Frank dreamed his dad was trying to reach him by phone. It rang and rang, but no one answered it. No matter how hard he tried,

Frank couldn't move. His arms were pinned beneath him, his mouth was locked shut. . . .

*Brriiing!*

Frank reached out and grabbed the phone off its hook. "Hello?" he said, his voice groggy and muffled.

"Rise and shine, lazybones!" a reply came.

Frank shot up in bed. Every last ounce of sleepiness had suddenly vanished.

"Who is it, Frank?" Joe asked, sitting up, too.

"Don't you think you fellows ought to get a move on?" The voice was warbly and mechanical, exactly like the one Frank had heard the day before.

"Who are you?" Frank blurted out.

The answer sent an icy chill up Frank's spine. "Don't waste your time with foolish questions. Your mother has only ten hours left to live."

# Chapter

## 6

BEFORE FRANK COULD SAY a word a sudden click sounded in his ear.

He slammed the phone down and shot to his feet. "We're out of here!"

"Was it *him?*" Joe asked, his face taut with disbelief.

"Believe it or not," Frank said, slinging his duffel bag over his shoulder.

Joe picked up his bag and followed Frank out the door. "How could he know where we were?"

"Remember what Mr. Congeniality in the motel office told us last night? This was the only place in Marfield with vacancies—and someone just happened to call asking about vacancies a few hours before we arrived. Guess who that must have been. It wouldn't take a genius to realize we'd be staying here.''

"Yeah, but there's one problem. How could that guy have known we were in Marfield—unless he bugged our backyard? That's the only place we talked about it!''

"Maybe not,'' Frank said, rushing down the concrete path to the motel office. "Maybe we talked about it in the van before we knew it was bugged.''

Joe shook his head. "No, Frank. I'd remember!''

"Or maybe they tailed us somehow.'' Frank's voice had an edge now. He was at the office door, and he turned to face his brother. "It doesn't matter, Joe, does it? The most important thing is to get Dad back to Bayport within ten hours. That means we have only about five hours to find him!''

With that he pulled open the screen door. The thin man was still behind the counter, but awake this time. On the wall behind him a clock read 7:45. "Yes, gentlemen, would you like a room?''

Frank put the key on the counter. "Uh, we have one already, sir. Remember? Last night? You were the one who gave us the key. We'd like to check out now.''

The man raised his eyebrows. "Ah, yes, of course!'' He looked at the keys and gave a little chuckle. "I gave you room J, eh? Oh, dear, I mustn't have been in a very good mood. Sorry about the sign, fellows." Giggling, he reached behind him for his receipt book.

"No problem," Joe said dryly. "It was very—colorful."

That made the man giggle even more. "Oh, yes, I'll bet it was!" He looked at the reservation card. "Please pay this amount, Peter—or are you Jules?"

"Huh?" Joe said.

"Peter," Frank quickly answered, remembering their aliases. He quickly counted out the money and put it on the counter. "Do you have a map of the area?"

Barely containing his mirth, the man took the money with one hand. With the other he pointed to a rack in the corner and turned away. As he went into an inner office behind the counter Frank could hear a little explosion of laughter.

"A comedian," Joe mumbled. "Let's get out of here, Peter."

"Okay, Jules," Frank replied. He grabbed a map from the rack and gave it to Joe. "You're appointed navigator."

They raced out to the van and jumped in. From the passenger seat Joe checked the map. "Hang a right," he said as Frank started up.

The van's rear wheels kicked up gravel.

Leaving the Marfield Motor Hotel behind gave
Frank and Joe a fleeting sense of relief that was
buried in a stronger, darker anxiety. It was a
feeling both boys shared but didn't dare speak
about.

For all their skills, they could never hope to
match the cunning of one other detective—
Fenton Hardy, their father. When Fenton decided to solve a crime no one could do it faster
or better.

And when Fenton Hardy decided to remain
incognito it was practically impossible for any
human being to find him.

"A cheerful little place," Joe said, looking
out the van window.

A jagged spiral of barbed wire glinted in the
morning sunlight on top of a grim, ten-foot-
high brick wall that stretched ahead of them
for a quarter mile. Frank followed it until he
came to a stop sign. There the otherwise solid
wall gave way to a metal gate. Beside the gate
was a Plexiglas booth with a small white-on-
black sign that read "Foreman Aerospace/Au-
thorized Personnel Only."

Frank turned into the gate, prompting the
guard in the booth to lean into his desk microphone.

"Can I help you?" The guard's voice
sounded distant and tinny as it squawked out

over a small loudspeaker next to Frank and Joe. Next to the loudspeaker was a grating with the words *Speak Here* printed underneath.

"Two cheeseburgers, one large fries, a root beer, and a shake," Joe said under his breath.

"I'm sorry," the voice returned.

Frank gave his brother a sharp glance. "Uh, we're here to see Fenton Hardy. We understand he's here on a business trip."

"Who's he visiting?" the guard asked.

"I'm not sure," Frank replied. "But he came in Thursday. I'm sure his name is on the sign-in sheet."

The loudspeaker fell silent for a few seconds. "No, I'm checking all the way back to Monday now, and I don't see any Hardy. That's *H-A-R-D-Y.*"

"Is it possible he could have gotten through another way?" Joe called out.

"No, sir. If the President of the United States came to visit, he'd have to come through this gate, just like you. I'm sorry, but I can't let you in. If there's someone inside you can call—"

"No, thanks," Frank said, cutting him off. "We'll call him at his office. I guess he hasn't left yet. But if he does show up, could you tell him to call the van immediately?"

"Just—the *van*, sir?"

"He'll know what it means. Thank you."

Frank backed onto the street, staring dully behind him.

"What if he's in there, Frank?" Joe said. "He could be using an alias, he could have pulled some strings . . ."

Frank heaved a sigh. "Let's try our luck at the other places before we start second-guessing."

Using the map, Joe guided Frank to the Center for Experimental Research, a boxy, ten-story office building made of glass and steel. They parked at the curb of the building's small, well-kept lawn and walked inside.

A guard stood behind a gray metal desk. On his green khaki uniform was a name tag that read "R. Muldoon." He doodled with a pen in the margins of a half-finished word-hunt game. A telephone and a closed sign-in book sat at one edge of the desk.

"Excuse me," Joe said, "we're here for a meeting with Fenton Hardy. Has he come in today?"

Muldoon didn't look up from his puzzle. "You got a clearance pass?"

"Uh, I'm sure Mr. Hardy will give us clearance. Would you check?"

"No clearance, no entry."

Frank stepped forward. "Can't you at least tell us if he's here?"

49

"No clearance, no entry." Muldoon circled a word that went diagonally across his puzzle.

Joe casually turned the sign-in book around to face him and started flipping through.

Instantly Muldoon's arm shot out and slammed the book shut. "Hey, what do you think this is, some kind of game? I got a job to do, understand? Now get out of here before I call the authorities!"

"Hey, I wouldn't want you to do that," Joe said, looking at him levelly. "You might lose your concentration—then you'd never see the word *defective* running down the right side of your puzzle."

Muldoon smacked his pen again. "That does it." He lifted the phone and said, "Muldoon here. I've got a situation four at the front desk."

Within seconds a tall, trim man with a mane of silver hair emerged from a door beside the elevators. Walking briskly toward them, he gave a calm, confident smile. "Gentlemen," he called out in a booming bass voice. "What can I do for you?"

"These guys are trying to get in here without no clearance, Mr. Straeger," Muldoon said.

"Without *any* clearance, Robert," the older man said. "Double negatives fell into disrepute after Shakespeare's time."

Muldoon frowned and looked back at his puzzle.

"Karl Straeger, head of security," the gray-haired man said. He gestured toward a corner of the lobby. "This way, please, gentlemen."

As the three of them walked over Frank said, "Sorry to cause confusion, Mr. Straeger, but we need to talk to Fenton Hardy immediately. We have reason to believe he's in a meeting here."

Straeger mulled over Frank's request. "Hardy—Hardy—the name isn't familiar."

"If you'd just let us look at the sign-in book," Joe insisted.

"Of course," Straeger said. "But I can tell you right now, all visitors' names are logged in my office, and I make it my job to learn every one. After thirty years in this business I've learned how to remember. I assure you that the person you mention has not entered this building."

"He told us he would be in an important research meeting," Frank insisted. "I'm sure this is the place he mentioned."

Straeger smiled. "Ah. He probably said the Center for *Environmental* Research. Often people confuse us. You see, we're not actually a research organization, but rather a clearing-house of sorts. We evaluate research proposals for the government."

Before Frank could reply, Straeger held up his hand. "It certainly isn't my job to make your search difficult, though. And in my advancing years my mind has been known to slip." He led them back to the desk, where he told Muldoon, "Let these two young men read the logbook."

With a wink Straeger walked back to his office.

Frank and Joe scoured the book's entries for the last week, but Straeger was right. Fenton Hardy had not signed in.

"What'd I tell you?" Muldoon grumbled as the brothers turned to walk away.

Next stop was Prometheus Computing, a small complex of squat brick buildings connected to one another. Over the entrance of the main building was a carving of a man chained to a rock on the top of a mountain. Above him vultures wheeled in the air, preparing to pounce. But the man was oblivious to them as he hunched over a computer and typed furiously. The word *Prometheus* was carved underneath him.

"The Beast would be at home here," Joe remarked.

As at Foreman Aerospace, the buildings were surrounded by a fence with a guard booth. Frank and Joe drove up to see a young uniformed guard fiddling with a laptop computer on his table.

*"Checkmate!"* the man shouted, punching his fist in the air.

"Uh, excuse us," Frank said.

The man's face reddened when he saw Frank and Joe. "Sorry. I just beat the machine at chess for the first time in my life!"

"Great," Frank said without enthusiasm. "Listen, we need to see a man named Fenton Hardy. Is he here today?"

The guard fell silent for a moment. His eyes darted from Frank to Joe. "May I ask why you're here?"

Joe practically lunged over to the driver's window. "He's here, isn't he?" he said, his voice charged with excitement and relief.

The man stared back warily. "Uh, just a minute. Don't go away." Keeping his eyes on Frank and Joe, he picked up a phone and mumbled something into it. He nodded twice, then hung up.

In front of them the gate swung open. "Take a right, then a left into courtyard B," the guard said.

Frank followed the instructions, coming to a solid metal gate marked B that lifted slowly. A quadrangle of grass was revealed, surrounded by four ivy-covered walls. It was completely empty.

From behind them another guard appeared as if from nowhere. "Go ahead," he urged. "Someone'll meet you inside."

Frank gave his brother an uncomfortable look. Joe shrugged back, and they drove inside.

The van jounced as it went over the grass. In the middle of the quadrangle Frank turned the engine off.

"What is this?" Joe asked, looking around. "Where's Da—"

They both spun around at a loud metallic *boom* behind them. The metal gate had crashed to the ground, sealing off the exit.

Then came the slapping noises. Each window in the building was being thrown open, and from the second floor up long ropes flopped to the ground.

"I think we have visitors," Frank said.

Suddenly the walls of the building came alive. Clutching the ropes, a dozen people rappeled downward. Within seconds they dropped to the ground and surrounded the van.

Frank gulped. The commando uniforms weren't very welcoming, nor were the flak vests and gas masks.

But the worst—definitely the worst—were the submachine guns pointed at their heads!

# Chapter
# 7

"COME OUT OF THAT VAN with your hands up!" a voice bellowed out of a small black speaker behind them. Then the echo off the courtyard walls spoke the same words again.

Frank and Joe reached for their door handles, but before they could open them one of the commandos had stepped forward. "What are you doing here?" he demanded.

Frank and Joe turned toward the man as he ripped off his gas mask in one easy gesture.

Joe's eyes widened. Frank felt his heart skip a beat.

Frank opened his mouth to speak, but all that came out was a puny-sounding "Dad?"

Fenton Hardy had a look that defied definition. It was amused and baffled and angry.

"What are we doing here?" Joe repeated. He shifted uncomfortably. "Well, uh, to tell you the truth, that's what we wanted to ask you."

A half smile crept across Mr. Hardy's face. He looked to his right and left and gave a hand signal. "It's all right," he said. "These are my sons."

Around him the black-clad figures slowly lowered their guns.

Frank and Joe nodded awkwardly to them as they climbed out of the van. Many of the guards mumbled greetings as they turned back toward the building.

"Special security force," Mr. Hardy said to Frank and Joe. "Not bad for a few days' training, eh?"

Before either of them could answer, another voice boomed in the courtyard. "May I ask what on earth's going on?"

To their left, an overweight man in a three-piece suit trotted awkwardly toward them on obviously flat feet. His face was red with exertion, and the bottom of his white shirt bulged from under his vest.

Mr. Hardy exhaled with resignation. "That's Winthrop, the security chief. He's still sore because the Prometheus top brass went over his head to hire me as an independent contractor." He turned to face the approaching man.

"False alarm, Mr. Winthrop. My boys decided to come for an unexpected visit."

"I see," Mr. Winthrop said, giving Frank and Joe a cursory nod. "Perhaps, Mr. Hardy, your little SWAT team is being a bit overzealous. Besides, I thought your agreement was to remain incognito."

Joe blurted out, "This is a family emergency, sir. Something has happened to our mother. We'll explain in a minute, Dad," he said, trying to reassure his father.

Fenton Hardy cocked an eyebrow at his son and wrinkled his forehead, but he knew he had to wait until Winthrop left for his explanation.

Mr. Winthrop fidgeted, looking from Fenton Hardy to his sons. He seemed to be trying to decide whether to be suspicious or sympathetic.

He made up his mind quickly when he saw the van.

Narrowing his eyes at Joe, he said, "It looks like you had a little trouble on the way here."

Joe looked back and cringed. In the haste to reach his dad he hadn't thought of the van's appearance. Its side, riddled with bullets from the previous evening's attack, looked as if it had come through a war zone.

While he searched for an alibi Mr. Hardy stepped in. "I'm surprised at you, fellas. When you said you bought a van at an auction, I didn't think it was going to look like *this!*"

"Sorry, Dad," Frank said, taking his lead. "We're still waiting for the shop to give us an estimate."

"Well, never mind," Mr. Hardy replied, urging his sons toward the van. "There are more important things to think about. Excuse us, Mr. Winthrop."

"Wait—you're not going to—just a minute!" Mr. Winthrop sputtered as the three Hardys jumped into the van. "I can't be responsible for all your personnel! Why, I don't even know them!"

"Introduce yourself!" Fenton Hardy called from the van with a grin. "I'm sure you'll all get along. I'll be back as soon as I can."

"This is highly irregular!" Mr. Winthrop shot back. "It's not in my contract to play nursemaid to your—your commando troops!"

Mr. Winthrop's final words were lost in the van's engine noise as Frank did a quick U-turn and headed toward the metal gate. Mr. Hardy pulled a remote-control device out of his pocket and aimed it out the windshield. As Frank sped through the opening gate he caught a final glimpse of a furious Mr. Winthrop in his rearview mirror.

\* \* \*

"So we figure they jabbed glass into our tire so they could get Mom." Frank and Joe had just finished detailing their mom's kidnapping and the events surrounding it. The van was on the highway heading south now. The boys had taped clear plastic over the open window so the trip back would at least be warm.

"All we can do is get back on time and hope for the best," Fenton Hardy said, looking at his wristwatch. "We'll make it if we don't hit traffic."

"Does any of this make sense to you, Dad?" Frank asked. "Could it have anything to do with whatever you're doing up here?"

Mr. Hardy nodded. "I'm sure it does. Prometheus is sitting on something very hot right now. One of their teams has devised a revolutionary computer chip using a new superconductive material. It'll make the most powerful chip of today look like a rusty abacus—*and* it'll be smaller and cheaper. 'Battlechip,' they call it. Hard to believe, but the future of artificial intelligence is right here in Marfield."

"And it was being guarded by good old Mr. Winthrop. No wonder the company hired you," Joe said, trying to get his dad to talk and keep his mind off his wife's kidnapping.

"Actually, Winthrop is one of the best around," Mr. Hardy said, "so when an intruder managed to get by his people in the research building, the head office got nervous. They called me the next day, and my arrival turned out to be just in time. We got there in the middle of a raid. We sent the goons running. They didn't know what had hit them."

"Did you find out who they were?" Frank asked.

Mr. Hardy shook his head. "As soon as they knew the odds were against them they left in a hurry. It was obviously a well-planned operation. The only clue we have is a couple of phone calls from the same voice that called you. He sounded like Frankenstein in a blender."

"That's the guy," Joe replied. "And whoever it is has been on our tail since we left Bayport. We did our best to shake him—ripped out his bug, took all kinds of crazy routes—"

"I guess it isn't too tough to track down a van with a left side that looks like Swiss cheese," Mr. Hardy said.

He fell silent for a moment, drumming his fingers on the dashboard. Above them loomed a large green-and-white sign that said "Springfield Next Four Exits." "Get off here," he whispered.

"In *Springfield?*" Frank asked, perplexed. "Dad, we don't have a whole lot of—"

"Never mind, Frank, just get off—*now!*"

The exit was only thirty yards ahead, and

the van was in the center lane. Frank flicked on his turn signal, changed lanes, and leaned into the exit ramp.

Behind them a fanfare of car horns heralded a silver Toyota doing the same thing.

"Uh-oh," Frank said under his breath.

"You can never be too careful," Mr. Hardy replied as the van plunged into the heart of the city.

"Now what?" Frank asked.

"Hang a left toward the train station," Mr. Hardy said.

Frank did as he was told and found himself in the middle of a traffic jam. Horns blared, and shoppers threaded their way between the stalled cars.

Unfazed, Fenton Hardy said, "I'll meet you in the parking garage across the street." He grabbed the door handle.

Frank glanced at a four-story building to the right, which had a sign reading "Train Parking." "We're taking the train?"

"No," Mr. Hardy answered. "Just try to shake this guy. Maybe he'll follow me, and I can lead him away from you. If you have to leave the van, do it. I'll find you."

With that, he opened the door and climbed out into the traffic.

"But, Dad—" Joe protested.

It was too late. Fenton Hardy had disappeared into the crowd of pedestrians. At that moment the traffic began to move. Frank inched into the right lane and rolled slowly toward the parking garage entrance.

As they turned into the driveway a mechanized gate swung open. All the spaces on the first floor were taken, but the lanes between the parked cars were wide open. Frank stepped on the gas.

They spiraled to the second level, then the third. Frank peeked into the rearview mirror.

Coming around the last turn was the Toyota, its windows tinted black.

"Can you make out the driver?" he asked Joe, who was looking in his sideview mirror at the Toyota.

"Not a chance," he said.

Frank accelerated as he took the turn to the fourth level—right into the path of a station wagon in the wrong lane.

Frank yanked his steering wheel to the right. With a *screee* of brakes the station wagon slammed into a ninety-degree skid.

It just missed the van, but now it sat broadside to the lanes, almost blocking both of them.

The Toyota roared around the last corner, and the driver slammed on his brakes. Joe gritted his teeth. Frank felt his eyes squint, anticipating a crash.

Spinning wildly, the Toyota smacked against

the right wall and came to a dead stop. Its left rear bumper nicked the front of the station wagon.

"Hey, what's going on here?" a voice shouted. The driver's door of the station wagon flew open.

Taking advantage of the situation, Frank took off. At the end of the lane was a down ramp marked by an exit sign with an arrow.

"I guess it's downhill from here," Joe said.

"Yeah, right into the traffic again," Frank replied. "You know, that Toyota isn't going to just hang back, and I'm definitely not in the mood for a shootout in crowded downtown Springfield."

Joe suddenly pointed. "There's a parking place!"

"So?"

"Let's ditch the van."

*"What?"*

"Remember what Dad said," Joe pressed. "It doesn't make sense to me, either, but you know Dad. He must have a reason."

Frank thought of protesting, but he knew Joe was right. He pulled into the spot. In an instant he and Joe were out of the van and sprinting down a nearby stairwell that led to the street.

On the first floor was a metal door with a long horizontal handle. Joe flung his body against it. The door crashed open onto the sidewalk.

"Which way?" Joe said.

Frank pointed right. "I think Dad went that way."

Frank and Joe both began to run on the sidewalk back toward the entrance to the garage.

Joe stopped short. Frank almost crashed into him. It took only a split-second to regain his balance. But when he did, his eyes widened in shock at the sight of the silver car lurching to a stop inches from them!

# Chapter

# 8

FRANK'S INSTINCTS TOOK OVER. He spun around and grabbed his brother's arm. "Come on!" he shouted.

Before they could take off they were stopped by the sound of a familiar voice. "Get in!"

They turned back to the car. Waving from the front seat was Fenton Hardy.

"Dad!" Joe said. "It's you!"

"Sorry if I scared you," Mr. Hardy said with a smile. "Silver was the only color they had. If you were on your toes, you'd have recognized that this is a Mazda, not a Toyota."

"Oh—right," Frank said, too relieved to be embarrassed. He ran around to the passenger side while Joe climbed in the back.

With a hum of acceleration Mr. Hardy pulled

into the traffic. "That's a great place," he said, nodding in the direction of the car-rental agency across the street. Above the front door was a sign that said "Mendez Rental: Spee-Dee Check-Out." "You just give them your credit card number, and by the time they fill out the form, that car's waiting."

"I'll have to remember that for future reference," Joe remarked.

Mr. Hardy laughed as he inched toward an intersection and turned right. "Any sign of our friends?"

Frank cautiously looked out the back window. A grin spread across his face. "Guess who just came to the intersection."

Joe turned just in time to see the silver Toyota turning left at the light, moving away from them.

The traffic was thinner on this street. They were finally moving faster than they could by walking. "I don't know what they're so nervous about—why they're trying to stop us," Fenton Hardy said with a bitter edge to his voice. "We're doing exactly what they want us to do."

Frank settled back in his seat. His dad was right—much as he hated to admit it. They were playing into the plan of a sadistic stranger. Someone who quite possibly held their mother's life in his hands.

At least they were out of danger now, Frank thought. All they had to do was get out of Springfield, get back on the highway, and make tracks for Bayport. He looked at his watch. It was half-past noon. The voice had called at five-thirty, so there were five hours left.

He sighed with relief. Judging from the ride up, five hours would probably do it.

At the end of the street an orange sign said "Construction Detour to Highway." It pointed to a narrow road on the right—a road brought to a standstill with stopped cars and trucks.

As their car ground to a halt Frank felt beads of sweat form at his hairline. He couldn't help looking at his watch again. Only thirty seconds had passed since the last time he checked, but this time the sight of it made his heart sink.

Five hours suddenly didn't seem like a whole lot of time.

When Fenton Hardy turned into the family driveway Joe almost fell out. In his eagerness he had pressed the door handle early.

On his watch the liquid crystal display read 5:41.

He managed to stay inside until Mr. Hardy braked to a sudden halt. Wordlessly, the three Hardys bolted out of the car and up the front lawn.

Joe fumbled for his keys, then unlocked the

door and pushed it open, nearly knocking it off its hinges. Another time the fact that the door had been fixed would be foremost on his mind. Another time he would have noticed that the house had been put back together. He should have been amused that Phil, Chet, and Biff were still there, gorging on a dinner cooked by Aunt Gertrude.

But none of those things registered much as he and Frank stormed into the kitchen. The words "Did anyone call?" flew out of his mouth.

"Nice to see you, too!" Phil said, his mouth full of spaghetti with white clam sauce.

"You're here, Fenton!" Aunt Gertrude exclaimed. "Thank goodness. I've been worried sick."

Biff let out a groan of mock disappointment. "You mean we're going to have to *share* the spaghetti?"

"Biff, this is important," Mr. Hardy said, entering the kitchen behind his sons. "We were expecting a call at five-thirty."

Chet looked at Phil, who looked at Biff. "Well, we were outside until just a minute ago. If the phone rang—"

"Aunt Gertrude, you were here, right?" Frank interrupted.

"Yes, I was," Gertrude replied, serving up three more plates of spaghetti. "And you did

68

get a call, right on the dot of five-thirty. It was
. . . beastly."

Frank felt his stomach churn. Beside him
Joe's shoulders slumped and Fenton Hardy
turned away.

"What do you mean?" Frank asked. "Sort
of garbled and electronic-sounding?"

Taking her ladle out of the pot of sauce, Aunt
Gertrude paused. For a moment her brow
scrunched with a puzzled expression. She
looked as if she was about to ask a question,
then stopped. A smile flashed across her face.
"No, no! That was the boy's name—Beastly!"

Now it was Frank's turn to be puzzled. He
looked around at Joe.

The younger Hardy's eyes lit up. "Biester!
Was that the name, Aunt Gertrude? Larry
*Biester?*"

Aunt Gertrude frowned as she reached for
the silverware drawer. "Oh. Yes, I suppose
that was it. A nice young man. He said he was
calling from Yale—"

"Harvard," Joe corrected.

"Well, you know, they're all the same to me.
He said he'd call back later." She brought two
of the plates to the table. "Scoot over, fellows.
I think the three Hardys deserve a place at
their own table."

"Gertrude," Mr. Hardy said, "I'm not very

hungry right now. I'd like Frank and Joe to show me exactly what happened here.''

With a loud sigh that clearly indicated her disapproval Aunt Gertrude said, "Fortunately, there's nothing to show. In case you hadn't noticed, the boys and I have tried to restore the house to a semblance of normality.''

"That's not true," Chet countered. Swallowing, he pointed to the den. "We saved the evidence in there.''

Mr. Hardy went into the den, followed by Frank, Joe, and Aunt Gertrude. In a neat pile in the center were pieces of the splintered door frame, which had been replaced; plaster from the hole in the living room wall; and the cloth bag and rope that had bound Aunt Gertrude.

Mr. Hardy rummaged through them, examining each item and placing it back in the pile. One of the broken shards of wood caught his eye, and he held it up. Caught in its jagged edges was a three-inch square of green material.

"Cotton twill," Mr. Hardy said, fingering it. "Did you catch a skirt on this, Gertrude?''

Aunt Gertrude looked insulted. "I don't own a skirt made of *that* material. That must be from the forest ranger's shirt.''

"The forest ranger?" Mr. Hardy repeated.

"Yes, the barbarian who tied me up! Didn't the boys tell you?''

Frank and Joe gave their father a meaningful look that said, "Drop it for now."

"I see," Mr. Hardy said. He put down the thread, then picked up the rope with two hands. "Hmmm. Must be quite some forest. There's an ocean in the middle of it."

"Huh?" Joe said.

Frank grabbed the rope and examined it. "Of course! It's nautical line, isn't it, Dad? The kind you use to tie a boat to a dock."

Mr. Hardy smiled. "Exactly."

"Exactly," Joe repeated with a shrug. "I knew that."

Mr. Hardy was about to say something when a telephone ring sliced through the air.

For a split second they all froze.

Mr. Hardy moved first. He ran into his office and grabbed the receiver. "Hello?" he said, practically shouting.

In the dead silence that followed he nodded vigorously to his sons. Frank and Joe bolted into the kitchen, where they picked up the phone and shared the earpiece.

"Who—" Chet began to say, but a look from Frank was enough to cut his sentence off in midstream.

"You will leave the second window from the left unlocked and disengaged from the alarm system," the electronic voice was saying. "Through this window you will drop three

71

Prometheus uniforms into the hedge. At exactly three-thirty P.M. you will report a bomb threat in the mailroom. Section Two is to be cleared of all personnel, giving access to the research building.''

"You must be out of your mind!" came Mr. Hardy's incredulous voice. "You expect *me* to let you into the building?" A strange, almost desperate laugh escaped from him. "No way, pal! You're going to have to do it yourself— over my dead body!"

"Yours?" the voice replied with a chilling undercurrent. There was a sudden clicking sound. The phone had not been hung up, but the electronic buzz that had accompanied the voice stopped. The silence hung heavy in the air.

"Fenton?"

It was Mrs. Hardy. "Mom!" Joe exclaimed before he could stop himself.

"These men—these men mean what they say, darling," she said.

Frank felt the blood drain from his face as the phone went dead.

# Chapter

## 9

FRANK'S HANDS WERE COILED around the phone receiver as if it were a lifeline to his mother. For a few seconds he and Joe could only stand, stunned.

When he finally did hang up Frank noticed that his knuckles were white.

He looked at Joe and saw an expression on his face he'd never seen before. Was it terror? Fear? Anger? He wasn't sure, but whatever it was, he knew he was feeling it, too. Nothing they'd experienced before—multimillion-dollar heists, terrorist threats, computer scams—none of them compared to the kidnapping of their mother.

Everything that needed to be said was in the brief glance the boys exchanged. Biff, Chet, and Phil must have sensed it, too, because they didn't say a word. They watched with silent respect as Frank and Joe walked back to their father's office.

"Is she all right?" Aunt Gertrude called after them.

Frank and Joe didn't hear the question, and they were only vaguely aware of Aunt Gertrude rushing into the room behind them. All three of them stood watching Fenton Hardy, waiting for his reaction.

He sat, looking down, rhythmically tapping his pen on a legal pad. When he raised his head his face was taut and composed.

"Dad?" Joe finally said.

Fenton Hardy met his son's gaze. His eyes were burning. Frank and Joe knew he had a plan.

But it would have to wait. The sudden, cold jangle of the phone stopped him before he could say a word.

His arm shot out for the receiver. "Hardy!" he said, almost shouting.

Frank and Joe watched his features relax a bit. "Oh, sorry, Larry. . . . Yes, I'm fine. . . . Well, it's a long story. I'll let you talk to him." He held out the phone to Frank. "It's the Beast."

"Larry," Frank said, grabbing the phone. "I'll call you back in five, okay?"

"Oh, sure, Frank," the Beast replied. "But it'll only take a sec—"

"Thanks," Frank cut in. "Don't go anywhere." He slammed the phone down.

"What'd you do that for?" Joe asked.

"I don't want to take any chances," Frank answered. "We found a bug in the wall, but how can we be sure they haven't tapped our phone line?"

"Good point," Mr. Hardy said. "But how did the Beast get involved in this?"

"We may have a lead on the owner of the car that attacked the van yesterday," Frank wrote on a piece of yellow lined paper. "I'm going to a pay phone." Then out loud he said, "Come on, Joe."

Frank and Joe ran out to the rented car and drove to Pie in the Sky, a pizza place five blocks from home. Through the window they could see it was crowded, but the pay phone by the door was unoccupied.

"Perfect," Frank said.

"I don't know, Frank," Joe replied, scanning the parking lot, which was full of cars coming and going. "Maybe I'm being paranoid, but at this point I wouldn't be surprised if someone was following us with a shotgun mike."

"That's why this place is so perfect. Even if

75

someone was parked right outside, he wouldn't pick us up over the crowd noise.''

By the time Joe parked Frank was already at the phone. He dialed Larry Beister's number.

"Hello, meester, this is Larry Biester!" came the Beast's voice.

"I think you've been sitting in front of a VDT too long," Frank replied. "It's warped your sense of humor."

"Ooh, you really know how to hurt a guy," the Beast said. "This is what I get for doing you a favor?"

"I take it back," Frank said with a laugh. "Did you get the info?"

"Hey, was there ever any doubt?" the Beast said triumphantly. "The plates are for a Buick registered under the name Todd Brewster, eighty-five Barrow Street, Marfield, Massachusetts."

"Todd Brewster, eighty-five Barrow Street," Frank repeated so that Joe could hear it. "Beister, you're a genius."

"Just do me one favor."

"What's that?"

"When it's all over, call and tell me what this was about."

"We'll come up and tell you in person," Frank said.

"Over a pot of my famous homemade baked beans!" the Beast added.

"On second thought, maybe we'll call."

With a laugh and a quick goodbye Frank hung up and raced back to the car.

In minutes Frank and Joe had returned to their house. They barged through the front door to see Mr. Hardy pacing the living room floor. Aunt Gertrude stood to the side, her face creased with concern. Biff, Chet, and Phil were nowhere to be seen.

"There's got to be a way to find her," he said without losing a step. "There was only about an hour between the time they took her and the time they called. They couldn't have gone far; my guess is they're still near Bayport."

"Dad," Joe said, "we found out the name of the guy who followed us. It's Todd Brewster, and he lives in Marfield."

Mr. Hardy stopped pacing. He cocked his head, deep in thought. "The name doesn't ring a bell, but it's a lead, and a strong one. One of us should go stake him out."

"I'll do it," Frank said.

"Good," Mr. Hardy replied. "I want to stick around to see if I can dig up anything about any newcomers in Bayport."

Joe was fiddling with the nautical rope, which Mr. Hardy had brought into the living room. "I'll check out the harbor area. Maybe they're hanging out down there."

"There's one problem," Frank said. "I know it's a rented car, I know we shook off a tail in Springfield, but they know we're here now. What if I'm followed to Massachusetts?"

Fenton nodded gravely. "I'll take care of it." He pulled a fistful of change out of his pocket and quickly examined it. "The phone company's going to love us today. Be back in a minute."

When Fenton Hardy returned from his drive to the pay phone he was carrying a sheet of paper with a hand-drawn map. He thrust it toward Frank. "Here's the way you'll get to Marfield. It's basically small highways all the way, with a couple of detours onto roads. Whatever you do, don't deviate from this route."

"Right," Frank said.

"And be sure to check in with Winthrop tomorrow."

"Right," Frank said again. He folded the map and put it in his pocket. After a quick goodbye he ran out to the car, armed with a cold soda and a couple of sandwiches that Aunt Gertrude had slipped him.

It was going to be a long ride.

\* \* \*

Halfway through Connecticut Frank was slowed down by a major accident and sat in traffic for over an hour while it was cleared. Following the route his father had given him, Frank had wound his way through the centers of many small towns.

Now Frank felt his eyelids getting heavy. The night's sleep at the Marfield Motor Hotel had obviously not been enough. He lifted his directions to eye level and stole a quick glance. He was to take the next exit and snake around a tiny town called Devaron, then get back on the highway at the next exit.

A tiny voice inside him grumbled that the trip would have been much faster if he had been able to stick to the highways.

Resignedly, he took the Devaron exit and made his way along a narrow, unlit road through a forest. On the winding turns his headlights shone white against the many tree trunks and bushes. Farther along there were clusters of small houses. Moments later the building gave way to forest again, and Frank realized he had gone through the town already. Below him weeds peeked out of the ruts. He felt as if no one had driven this way in months.

As the road straightened out he found himself hoping for an all-night gas station or convenience store where he could pick up something to drink. Maybe around the next bend . . .

Frank sped into the next turn faster than he had intended. The curve continued for more than 150 degrees. His tires screamed as the car listed to the left.

When the road finally straightened out Frank was only riding two wheels—both on the left side. The first thing he saw in his headlights was four people, all dressed in blue, diving for the side of the road. Then he saw the flashing lights.

Frank's foot hit the brake as the car fell back on four wheels. He registered that there was something ahead of him, blocking his way. As he skidded from side to side Frank made out what the lights were for, and why those people were dressed in blue.

He was zigzagging straight at a police road-block!

# Chapter

# 10

THE SOUND of Frank's tires screeching grew louder and louder. Through the windshield the light blue sawhorses loomed larger, as if they were growing in crazy time-lapse photos. Behind the sawhorses two police cars were parked nose to nose, their lights flashing. Frank clenched his jaw and waited for the crash.

His fingers were locked around the steering wheel. His teeth were bared, and his eyes were closed to shut out the moment of impact. But there was no crash. His brakes held.

When Frank opened his eyes the bright white message "Property of Devaron Police Dept." painted on a blue sawhorse was about three quarters of an inch from his front grille.

"Couldn't you get it a little closer?" came a gruff voice from the side of the road.

Frank spun around to see a broad-shouldered policeman strolling toward him. The reality of the situation came flooding back. Here he was on a strange road in the middle of northern Connecticut, dead tired at ten o'clock, trying to track down a man who might be following him. Now he was about to go to jail for almost wiping out an entire small-town police department. "Sorry, officer," he said.

"You'll be even sorrier if you don't have your license and registration," the officer answered. Behind him three other officers stood impassively by the side of the road.

Frank took his license out of his wallet and opened the glove compartment for the rental registration. He handed them over. "I didn't expect something like this in the middle of—" He stopped himself, guarding his choice of words in an unfamiliar neighborhood.

"Nowhere? Is that what you were going to say?" The officer leaned down and pushed his face through Frank's window. There was a grin across his stubbled face.

"Well, I don't see roadblocks anywhere too often," Frank replied. He could see the other police officers sauntering closer.

The officer nodded silently. Frank fidgeted

as the man's coal black eyes bore down on him. "You look a lot like your dad," he finally said.

Frank was sure he hadn't heard right. "Uh, excuse me?"

The officer stood and turned to the others. "Fenton Hardy's son. Pretty good resemblance, huh?"

Smiling, they nodded in agreement. Frank felt completely bewildered. "What's going on here? How do you know my dad?"

The officer stuck his hand out toward Frank. "Henry Singer, chief of Devaron Police. I'm an old colleague of your dad's from way back when we were on the New York City police force. He called a few hours back to warn me you'd be coming through here and might have a tagalong breathing down your neck. I told him to route you along this road and I'd make sure you got to Marfield alone."

In front of him one of the officers had climbed into a police car, and another was moving a sawhorse away.

Frank's grin now mirrored Officer Singer's. "Thanks," he said as a feeling of relief washed away his tension.

"All right, now, why don't you pull over to the side?"

Frank felt a shudder of dread. Was he going to give him a ticket after all?

Officer Singer seemed to read Frank's mind. "Don't worry. I brought my car for you to use." He indicated a small Firebird resting on the right shoulder. "In case anyone *is* after you, this'll really throw them off. This car will be okay. Your dad gave me the address of the rental place, and I'll have one of my rookies return it tomorrow."

"But—your own car? I can't—"

"I've been trying to sell it for weeks," Officer Singer said, chuckling. "Hey, if you like it, maybe you can make me an offer."

Frank maneuvered his car to the side and got out. "I'll talk to my dad about it."

As Frank got in and started it up Officer Singer gave him a little salute. "Say hello to him for me," he said.

"You bet," Frank replied. He shifted into gear as the police car moved away, clearing the road.

"One other thing," Officer Singer added as Frank started off.

Frank stopped again and looked back out the window.

"Uh, keep it under the speed limit, okay, buddy?" the officer said with a wink.

Frank smiled and pulled away, obeying the advice.

Turning left around the next bend, he thought he could hear the screech of tires. It might have come from the highway, which he could see in the distance—or it might have come from behind him. But when he looked into his rearview mirror the roadblock was out of sight.

Either way, Frank had a good feeling as he drove up the ramp to the highway—a feeling that he was definitely on his own.

Number 85 looked like all the other houses on Barrow Street—two stories, white shingles, a sloping roof with a dormer, and a screened-in porch. In front there were neat hedges and a well-kept lawn. Sort of a disappointment, Frank thought. So average and unthreatening.

Except for what was parked in the driveway, that is. The outline of the familiar Buick sat there, its black-tinted windows shut for the night, its license number, NZE-809, the same that he had seen the night before.

Frank looked carefully at the house. Whoever this Todd Brewster was, he was asleep.

Which was good, as far as Frank was concerned. He nestled himself into as comfortable position as he could. It wasn't his bedroom, but it felt a whole lot better than driving. In fact, it felt pretty terrific at that moment. As he drifted into sleep he thought that maybe he *would* ask his dad to make Officer Singer an offer on the car.

The next thing Frank knew, he was squirming under the heat of some kind of spotlight. He didn't know where he was, or how he had gotten there. He was only aware of intense orange light that was making his head throb and his neck ache.

Leering down at him was Todd Brewster. He had never seen the man, but somehow he *knew* it was him. Brewster's lean face looked like a skull with a thin layer of flesh. Behind him, screaming as she was engulfed by flames, was Laura Hardy. Frank tried to go after her but couldn't move. He tried to yell, but his mouth was frozen. A sharp, paralyzing pain began to shoot down his neck, spreading to his shoulders. . . .

Frank's eyes flew open. A startled gasp escaped from his mouth. He squinted at the early-morning sun that was framed by his windshield.

Of course. He had parked facing east, and in his dream the rising sun had become a spotlight.

He grabbed his neck, which had stiffened during the night and now throbbed with pain. The nightmare was over, but waking up was no joy. He had to get out, walk around, shake out the cobwebs.

But the moment he grabbed the door handle he froze. Across the street a screen door had slammed. He looked out his window.

An athletic-looking blond man walked out of 85 Barrow Street. He was about six foot one, and he wore a neatly pressed dark suit. There was a leather briefcase in his left hand. With his right hand he waved to a neighbor and shouted a friendly greeting.

" 'Morning, Todd," the neighbor called as Brewster climbed into the Buick.

Frank felt a twinge of relief that Todd Brewster was not the cadaverous man he'd seen in his dream. In fact, Brewster's most outstanding characteristic was that he was so *average*. He was about the last person Frank would expect to be a hit man.

Frank waited until Brewster was a block away before he started up the Firebird. He followed him through the suburban streets and onto a busy main thoroughfare.

As the sun streamed in through his window Frank put down the visor and stifled a yawn. He had a sense of déjà vu about this street, but it left as quickly as it had come.

Brewster turned off the main road and onto a long street that curved sharply left. For a few moments Frank lost him, and his heart started to race.

But when he came around the bend he saw Brewster's car up ahead. Suddenly Frank knew where his déjà vu had come from.

He had been here before—the Marfield Center for Experimental Research!

# Chapter

## 11

THAT SAME MORNING, Joe walked along the Bayport harbor. He glanced at the sheet of paper his dad had given him and read "Captain Claes Rymond, Scandinavian Shipping, Slip 7" once again.

The ships started at number four. Where the first three had been there was now an enormous parking lot. A high concrete wall had been built along the southern edge of the lot and painted with a multicolored mural to hide the blighted docks. Joe had seen photos of the Bayport waterfront fifty years earlier, and it had swarmed with barges, ferries, steamers, and other trade ships. Longshoremen toted boxes and sacks from the ships to the warehouses just inland. Nowadays only four hulking wooden docks remained, each topped with a cracked concrete walkway, and each looking as if it were about to fall into the inlet.

The warehouses that hadn't been torn down were dilapidated, and only half were in use. One of them was marked with a rusted metal sign that said SC NDI AVI N HIPPIN .

Joe knocked three times on the front door, which was paneled with riveted metal sheets. He heard four hollow reports echo within the building and wondered if it was empty.

He was about to knock again when the door started to creak open. Out of the darkness within two small eyes glowed. Joe was faintly aware of a sweet burning smell.

"Yeah?" came a hoarse, reedy voice.

"J-Joe Hardy." Joe couldn't help feeling a little nervous.

The door opened all the way, revealing a short, hunched man with enormous shoulders. He continued looking at Joe through slitted eyes and sent out a puff of musty, fragrant smoke from the pipe in his mouth.

"Fenton's boy. Yeah, come in," he said in a barely audible mumble. "I'm Rymond, but you can call me Captain Claes."

As Joe followed him the clack-clack of their footsteps resounded through a room that stretched up at least fifty feet. Occasional bare light bulbs threw small pools of illumination every few feet. Aside from three clusters of boxes marked "Fragile" in one of the corners and a collection of tools on wall hooks, the room seemed almost empty to Joe.

The captain led Joe to a sturdy-looking wooden desk against the opposite wall. He plopped down in a green leather armchair, and Joe pulled up a folding chair.

"Captain Claes," Joe began, "as my father may have told you, I'm checking for any newcomers to this area—anyone who might own this rope or wear a shirt made of this material." He held out the nautical rope and green thread.

Captain Claes examined the two specimens and puffed on his pipe again. "I've seen this rope, all right—on just about every boat that's ever come through here. As for the thread, well, when I meet a fella I don't usually pay much attention to his wardrobe. That's just the way I am."

Joe could see he wasn't going to be any great help. "No unusual ships have come through?"

The captain thought for a moment. "Mike Merwin's tramp steamer, a couple of barge tugs. No, but I know those guys like I know me." He shook his head. "Nope, guess I can't help you."

"Okay, thanks." Joe sprang from his seat and began heading for the door, happy to be leaving. But Captain Claes's voice stopped him.

"You might try the marina, young fella. Seems there's a heck of a lot more pleasure craft these days than trade ships. Look up Paul Douglas in Bayport Marine Supplies. He keeps his eye on everything over there."

Bayport Marine Supplies was a sprawling glass building overlooking the marina, which was thriving with activity.

Joe quickly found Paul Douglas, a silver-haired, mustached man, behind the cash register. When he described what he was looking for Mr. Douglas looked at him as if he were crazy.

He repeated Joe's request. "You want to track down someone who just arrived at the marina? Is that all you're going to tell me? What color is his hair? How old? Is he bigger than a bread box?"

"The trouble is, I don't know," Joe said with exasperation. "But I'm sure most of the boat owners come in here a lot. Wouldn't you notice if someone a little . . . unusual started hanging around?"

Mr. Douglas looked out the window and drummed his fingers on the counter. "You know, there *is* that yacht that pulled in the other day. The guys on board haven't stopped

in here yet. I don't think they're too friendly."
He gave a short, sniffling laugh. "Either that
or they're trying to hide something."

Joe's eyes lit up. *Now* they were getting
somewhere. "What do you mean, 'hide something'? How can you tell?"

Mr. Douglas shrugged. "Hey, I'm only
shooting off my mouth, but it seems kind of
strange that they've docked so far out in the
harbor." He gestured out the window with his
arm. "You can barely see them. Can't figure
out why those guys don't come in closer;
there's plenty of spots this time of year. Maybe
they like their privacy."

"You said 'guys,'" Joe pressed. "Have you
seen them?"

"Well, two of them did come ashore once
the other evening in a big old powerboat. They
went to the grocery store and then right back
out to the ship again." He looked toward the
door and nodded to a young couple who had
just walked in.

"Do you remember what they looked like?"

Now Mr. Douglas was beginning to get annoyed. "Hey, what is this? The third degree?
No, I don't remember what they looked like.
Look, if you'd like to buy something, be my
guest. But if not, I'd be happy if you'd let me
do my business here, all right?"

Joe pointed to a rack of fishing rods along the wall. "I'll take two of those," he said.

Mr. Douglas smiled. "Okay, now we're talking."

Joe paced the dock impatiently, dragging the fishing rods along the wooden slats. He was about to check his watch for the tenth time when Tony Prito walked up beside him.

"Tony!" Joe called out. "What took you so long?"

"Hey, give be a break," Tony replied. "You only called fifteen minutes ago. I thought I did pretty well, considering I had to search around the house for my dad's binoculars."

He was holding the binoculars in one hand and a floppy, plaid porkpie hat in the other. When he put it on his head the brim sagged down over his eyes and ears. "My fishing hat," he said with a grin. "How do I look?"

"Like a dweeb. It's perfect."

"Thank you. Here's yours." He held out a wide-brimmed fedora with the hatband missing.

"Leather," Joe said flatly, running his fingers over the water-stained cowhide. "This'll be nice and cool." He put it on and immediately felt sweat form on his brow.

"Well, at least the mystery kidnappers won't

see our faces," Tony remarked. "Did you rent a boat?"

Joe nodded and led him to a small motorboat tied to the dock near Bayport Marine Supplies. The rods he had bought sat on the floor.

"Where's the bait?" Tony asked, climbing in.

Joe gave him a sharp look. "This isn't a *real* fishing trip, Tony, remember?" He stepped into the boat and pulled the motor's starter. "It's more of a big-game hunt."

The engine roared to life. Joe throttled it down and steered the boat into the marina, taking a course to the right of the mysterious yacht. As they drew closer Tony remarked, "Wow. I thought they stopped making these after World War Two."

The boat was hulking and weather-worn, with patches on the side and an array of antennae and disks on deck. Joe was itching to use the binoculars. He cut the engine and tossed Tony a fishing rod. "Okay," he said. "Let's see what's biting."

They quickly cast their rods. While Tony pretended to troll for fish Joe propped his rod against the side of the boat with his leg. Then he held the binoculars to his eyes and aimed them at the yacht.

"It's old-fashioned, all right," Joe said. "It has steam engines instead of diesel. But take a look at the electronic equipment." He handed the binoculars to Tony.

Tony let out a low whistle. "Looks like they borrowed it from the space shuttle."

"It's state-of-the-art stuff," Joe said, taking the glasses back. "Satellite communications, radar—looks almost like a spy ship."

"No kidding," Tony said in awe.

Just then a flash of light caught Joe's attention. At first he thought it was glare off one of the ship's metal disks. But when he aimed his binoculars at the source he realized he was wrong.

It was another pair of binoculars, focused straight at him.

"Uh-oh," he muttered.

The whine of an outboard motor broke the peaceful silence. A powerboat was racing toward them from behind the yacht. Joe quickly stashed the binoculars under his seat and grabbed his fishing rod.

The boat didn't slow down as it approached. Instead it aimed straight for the stern of the small motorboat.

Tony's look said it all. "What is this dude trying to prove?"

The powerboat began circling Joe and Tony's boat counterclockwise, once—twice. It picked up speed, making its circle tighter and tighter.

In its wake Joe and Tony's boat pitched up

and down violently. The fishing rods clattered
to the deck.

"We're going to capsize!" Tony shouted.

"Hang on!" Joe shouted back, clinging to
the side.

"*What does he want?*" Tony's voice had
become a terrified wail.

As if in answer, the powerboat slowed down
and sliced back toward the yacht.

From its deck a man in a windbreaker leaned
out with a megaphone.

"Better stay away, kids," his voice blared.
"Or next time we go *through* your boat!"

# Chapter

# 12

"SEE YOU LATER, HONEY," the man said, leaning in the driver's window of the station wagon.

Frank stiffened at the sound of the voice. It was Muldoon, the guard who had stopped him and Joe the day before in the lobby of the Center for Experimental Research. He was saying goodbye to his wife. In his right hand was a small box wrapped in birthday gift paper.

Frank ducked behind his car, pretending to check his tires. When he looked back up the station wagon was gone, and Muldoon was walking through the front door of the building.

It wasn't going to be easy getting in past Muldoon.

Frank left the car and began sauntering toward the back of the building. The center sat on a slope, at the bottom of which was a truck dock—and, Frank hoped, an entrance.

Walking downhill, he kept the dark-tinted windows of the center's first floor in his peripheral vision. They were all lit by overhead fluorescents, except for one that was pitch-dark. He was surprised to hear a flurry of whispers drift out of the dark room's half-opened window. He considered turning and walking around the building the other way.

Suddenly the lights in that office flickered on, and a chorus of "Happy Birthday" blasted out. Frank gave a glance and saw Muldoon, Todd Brewster, and a couple dozen others singing to an embarrassed-looking red-haired woman.

If he was going to get inside, this would be the perfect time. He ran to the truck dock.

There was a door there, a heavy steel door with no handle. Frank tried to pry the door open with his fingers, but it was obviously locked. The sliding truck doors were padlocked, too.

Frank ran a few feet to his right and looked around the corner to the back of the building. A solid wall of glass and steel stretched across its entire length.

He decided to try the front door. As long as Muldoon was in the party room, Frank might be able to bluff his way in.

He had gone only a few steps when the steel door burst open. Thinking fast, he ducked behind a large white trailer that was parked at the dock.

"I can't believe she didn't know!" came someone's voice.

"She told me it was a total surprise." That voice was Muldoon's—and it was coming closer.

Frank felt the trailer begin to rock. Startled, he backed away. Did they know he was there?

From within the trailer a jumble of male voices was heard. He caught a few snatches: "Where's my shirt?" and "I knew they wouldn't get that oil stain out!" and "They really shrunk this thing!"

Frank realized the truck was used as some sort of makeshift dressing room. Suddenly it was clear to him how he could get into the center.

He waited for the men to leave, listening for the click of the metal door. Then he sprang into action, darting across to the front of the trailer. He reached out to test the doorknob.

It clicked open. Frank climbed inside and shut the door behind him.

He scanned the shelves along the wall, which contained neat stacks of kitchen whites, lab coats, and janitor uniforms. Then his eyes fell on a heavily starched and folded guard uniform. He picked up the shirt, letting the sleeves drop down. It looked as if he was in luck—it was about his size, maybe a little big. The right sleeve was—ripped!

*And the uniform was green.*

Green cotton twill. Frank smiled. He had found Aunt Gertrude's "forest ranger." So one of the guys who kidnapped his mother worked at the Center for Experimental Research.

Quickly Frank changed into the uniform, stashing his jeans, T-shirt, and jacket in a large plastic hamper.

He stepped out of the trailer and walked to the front of the building. Just as Frank had hoped, Muldoon was hard at work on a crossword puzzle. Without looking up he grunted a greeting as Frank walked by.

Walking quickly and purposefully through the lobby, Frank headed for the elevator and pressed the UP button. Behind him a few workers crossed from one hallway to the next. Frank paced back and forth, stealing a glance into the office next to the elevators, the room from which the security chief had emerged the day before. On the door were the words "Security/K. Straeger."

Just as he was about to peer in, the elevator door opened. Frank took a second to look inside the office—no one was there. He glanced over his shoulder. The lobby was empty, too.

Silently he slipped into the security office. Maybe there he could find answers to some of his questions—like what kind of organization the center was and where Brewster fit into it.

He found himself in a small outer office with a bulky wooden desk and four tall filing cabinets. Behind the desk was a locked door, probably leading to an inner office. He opened a file cabinet at random and began leafing through a folder marked "Correspondence." The first letter he saw was pretty boring: something about a service contract for an alarm system. As he put it back his eyes swept across the letterhead: Straeger Security, Subsidiary of MUX.

Frank's jaw dropped open. The name MUX was all too familiar. He hadn't expected to encounter that organization again—at least not with the same name. It had been a multinational front for a band of technology pirates in New York City, and he and Joe had sent them packing. The last Frank had heard, the leaders had been exiled overseas.

Now they were back, their tactics slimier than ever.

The click of footsteps on the marble lobby floor alerted Frank to someone approaching. He tucked the letter back into the file cabinet, closed it, and dived under the desk.

Frank could see two pairs of shiny black

shoes enter the room. They stopped at the door, and Frank heard it click shut. Then he heard the unmistakable voice of Karl Straeger:

"If all continues to go well, we'll achieve our goal this evening."

"But what about Hardy?" a younger man's voice piped up. "You told me he wasn't cooperating."

"Fenton Hardy will have no choice, of course. Matyus is giving him a chance to stew a little, to think about the consequences of his stubbornness, to imagine the horrible things that might be happening to his beloved wife. I think he'll cooperate very soon. I've decided the raid is to be at three o'clock at Prometheus—with or without Hardy's help."

"I don't think it's a good idea to wait. What if he goes after Matyus?"

"I'm sure he's spent every waking hour trying." He chuckled. "But his chances of finding the *Iron Maiden* are slim, and even if he did, its defenses are state-of-the-art."

The *Iron Maiden*. Frank had no idea what Straeger was talking about, but if he could call his dad—

"So where do I fit in?" the younger man queried.

"You are to lead the raid at Prometheus at precisely three o'clock. By that time I'll have flown to Bayport. You'll supervise the transport of the merchandise to me at the *Iron Maiden*, which sits far out in Bayport Harbor. Then, provided all has gone well, we'll take care of our—ah—collateral.''

Frank shuddered. So that was it. His mother was being held on a ship in Bayport Harbor! Did his dad know? Was it possible he or Joe could have found out? It didn't seem likely.

He had to get to a phone as soon as Straeger and his sidekick left.

But they didn't head out the doorway. Instead they circled around the desk, Straeger beside the young man. Frank saw the back of his trousers, then his shirt, then the silvery mane.

Don't turn around! Frank thought. If Straeger angled a couple of degrees to his right and looked down, Frank would be caught.

There was a jangle of keys. The door to the inner office swung open. Then, as quickly as they had arrived, Straeger and his young assistant disappeared into the other room.

Frank wasted no time. He scrambled out from under the desk and across the office to the outer door. Carefully he leaned against it and slowly turned the doorknob. It squeaked as he pushed it open—a tiny noise, but it sounded like a siren to him. He slid through, casting a final glance over his shoulder.

When he was in the lobby he pushed the

door shut and heaved a sigh of relief. He was safe.

Or so he thought.

"Hey, you!" an angry voice barked from across the hallway.

Frank wheeled around to see a guard approaching him—Todd Brewster!

"What can I do for you?" were the first words that came out of Frank's mouth.

"For one thing," Brewster retorted, "you can tell me what you're doing in my uniform!"

# Chapter

# 13

GLIDING AWAY from the dock in a rented Laser sailboat, Joe adjusted his sail and tacked right. He had dropped Tony and the powerboat off and checked in with his dad before renting the Laser.

The steady wind filled his sail, and he picked up speed. The tide was coming in, and the water was high; he wouldn't need to worry about sandbars. He looked left to see the old yacht fading in the distance. Tacking back and forth, he set a circular course around the yacht, well out of its sight.

Before long he could barely see the dock. He was out past the yacht, just short of the narrow inlet that led to open ocean.

There he dropped anchor.

"Time for a costume change," he said under his breath. He reached under his seat for the wet suit he had rented and slipped it on with his oxygen tanks. Fitting his mask into place, he rolled off the boat into the water.

He swam underwater toward the yacht, letting the incoming tide do most of the work. The thrum of the engines guided him, and in minutes he saw the ship's dark hull just before him.

Hang on, Mom, he thought. I'm almost there.

Joe was suddenly gripped by doubts. What if his mother wasn't aboard? What if the yacht had nothing to do with the kidnapping? Maybe it *was* a spy ship, or just some rich electronics whiz who treasured his privacy. Were the kidnappers holding his mother somewhere else?

And if the yacht did belong to the kidnappers, what then? A wet suit was great against the cold and wet, but it wasn't going to be much help against bullets.

Joe propelled himself forward, trying to cast those thoughts from his head. He swam alongside the starboard hull toward the stern. There he saw a long, taut anchor cable angling down and out of sight.

He followed it to the surface and emerged. The yacht was larger than it looked from a distance—at least fifty feet. There was no sound coming from the deck, but he wasn't high enough to see it.

He hoisted himself up the cable. The ship listed slightly with his weight, and Joe felt dread run down his spine.

No one seemed to notice. Joe swung his legs over and found himself on a secluded section of the yacht behind the wheelhouse. He silently removed his flippers and tanks, stashing them behind a stack of canvas folding chairs. Then he tiptoed across the deck toward some stairs. All around him the network of antennae felt like a spindly steel forest.

He looked down the stairwell. There was a well-lit hallway at the bottom but no sign of life.

The metal stairs felt icy cold on his bare feet as he climbed down. At the bottom the narrow corridor was lit by a string of bare light bulbs hanging from a jury-rigged electrical cord. The stark white walls were scuffed and dirty.

Some yacht, Joe thought. It was more like a prison barge.

He walked slowly down the corridor, his feet vibrating from the low, monotonous hum coming from the engine room. The door to the room was half-open. Eyeing it carefully, Joe walked slowly toward it. The doors to his left and right were closed.

He had a feeling that if his mother was on the boat, she'd be somewhere down there.

He reached out to the door on the left. Slowly he curled his fingers around the knob and, bracing himself, pushed it in.

Stacks of cardboard boxes greeted him. Some were open, revealing cans of food, first-aid supplies, housewares, and books.

Joe shut the door and turned to the one across the hall. He could hear something inside—a rustling of papers; the crackle of radio static, maybe. Again he twisted the doorknob gently—slowly—

The latch made a hollow pop as he pushed the door open.

"Captain?" a gritty voice called out.

A chair scraped on the floor. Through the crack between the door and the frame Joe could see a pistol lying on a table across the room. He knew he couldn't get to it first; it was too far away.

He turned and ran into the engine room. As he pulled the door shut behind him he heard the clatter of footsteps in the hallway.

"Captain?" the voice repeated.

Now the mechanical hum from the engines closed around him like the noise from a nest of giant bionic wasps. Behind him a network of steam pipes stretched from floor to ceiling. He backed away from the door, looking for a place to hide.

There were more footsteps, all coming closer. Joe dived behind a dense thicket of gears and pulleys in the middle of the room.

The door swung open. Light poured in again, outlining the broad silhouette of a man. Joe waited, rock-still, as the shadow passed from left to right and disappeared into a corner of the room.

Instinctively Joe backed off to his left, making sure to stay out of sight.

A flash of searing pain ripped through him. A scream exploded upward into his throat, where he caught it and choked it back. There was a faint smell of burning rubber. For an agonizing moment his eyes saw a mottled pattern of red and black.

He spun around, his teeth clenched, and saw that he'd backed right into one of the steam pipes. A small section of rubber wet suit clung to the spot, melting.

From the opposite corner of the room he heard the voice. "What do you think I did, chewed my way through the metal?"

The shock of recognition made Joe forget his pain. It was his mother's voice!

"I left the door open so I could hear you," the male voice said.

"And it shut when the ship rocked," Mrs.

Hardy said matter-of-factly. "It's not the first time it happened."

The shadow began to move left again. Without answering, the man walked out of the room, leaving the door ajar.

Joe waited for the footsteps to recede, then sprinted around the machinery.

Trapped like an animal in a locked metal cell, Mrs. Hardy looked up.

"Mom!" Joe whispered.

"Joseph Hardy," his mother said, "that was the riskiest, most wrongheaded thing you've ever done." She smiled. "And I'm proud of you."

"Don't talk too soon," he said. "We have to figure out how to get you out of here."

Mrs. Hardy gripped the steel bars and peered out at her son. "It isn't going to be easy to get through this," she said.

Anger welled up in Joe. He looked around for something to help him open the door. Next to the cell was a metal table stacked with magazines. It might have made a good battering ram if it hadn't been bolted to the floor. Above them a cardboard box marked "Stemware" stood on a shelf. The side was ripped, exposing a small circle of glass. That wouldn't help, either.

"They told me your dad agreed to do what

they wanted," Mrs. Hardy said ruefully. "Is that true?"

"I don't know," Joe answered. "That last time I talked to him—"

He was cut off by the sound of feet in the corridor.

"Hide!" Mrs. Hardy whispered. She grabbed a magazine and pretended to read it.

Joe dived behind the machinery, making sure to avoid the steam pipe.

With a heavy metallic clank the door crashed open. Footsteps thumped into the room, and a deep voice said, "Where is he?"

There was a momentary silence. "I beg your pardon?" Mrs. Hardy replied. "Where is *who?*"

"The young man in the wetsuit!"

Joe cringed. How could they have seen him? Closed-circuit TV? Joe immediately thought of the ripped stemware box. That wasn't the bottom of a glass sticking out—it was the lens of a camera! How could he have been so stupid?

He leaned to the left, hoping to see a path of escape. He could feel the heat of the steam pipes radiating behind him.

"I don't know what you're talking about," Mrs. Hardy said.

Joe slowly peered around the machinery. He could see a clock on the wall that said five after two, then the edge of the door.

"Captain Matyus, looks like we didn't get rid of all the mice on board!"

A red-haired man stepped into Joe's line of sight. Joe looked up into his face, which was twisted into an unfriendly grin.

"A mouse, eh?" the deep voice of a man who must have been Captain Matyus said. The redheaded man laughed and stepped out of the captain's way. Joe began to get up.

By the time he was on his feet he was staring down the barrel of a revolver. Holding his finger on the trigger was the captain, a burly man with a salt-and-pepper beard and the physique of an aging prizefighter.

"Looks more like a rat to me," Captain Matyus remarked. "It's too bad these mammals think with their emotions and not their brains. No matter what happens, they can always find their mothers."

"You sound just as phony as you did over the scrambler," Joe shot back.

"Ah, well," Captain Matyus said, ignoring Joe, "let's not let his efforts go unrewarded, gentlemen." He motioned Joe toward Mrs. Hardy with his pistol. As Joe walked across the room the red-haired man pushed him into the cage and locked it. Then he walked into the hallway, where four other men were peeking in.

Captain Martus backed into the doorway and

grabbed the knob. "Quite a lovely family re-union. I must call Fenton Hardy and tell him about it," he said to the others just before he pulled the door shut. "I hope the brig will be cozy enough for the two of you. If it's not, don't worry. I don't believe either of you will be with us that much longer."

# Chapter
## 14

"*YOUR* UNIFORM?" Frank said indignantly. "Just because we wear the same size, it doesn't mean—"

"Mr. Hardy!"

Frank spun around at the sound of Karl Straeger's voice. The silver-haired man stood in the doorway of the security office, smiling benignly.

"Remarkable that you got a job with us so quickly," Straeger continued. "And what a coincidence that you ripped your sleeve in the same place that Mr. Brewster did."

"Who are you, Straeger?" Frank said. "Or is that some sort of made-up name that MUX gave you?"

Straeger raised his eyebrows. "Well, it looks

as if you've been doing a bit of research, have you? Perhaps we should have a talk." He gestured toward his office. "Come in. I believe you know the way around."

Before Frank could step toward the office Brewster gave him a shove. Frank stumbled and caught himself against the doorjamb.

"Curb your aggressions, Todd," Mr. Straeger snapped. He looked at Frank and shrugged. "He has a tendency toward violence, you see—and an unfortunate, murderous temper. Which can be a bit embarrassing but is often quite handy. Although I have an agreement to report all antisocial acts to his parole officer, Todd and I have an agreement of our own."

Brewster gave a low chuckle. "You make me sound like some kind of animal."

"I can see MUX is doing its usual job of hiring only the best," Frank said, calmly walking into the inner office and finding Straeger's assistant, a short man, waiting there.

Brewster turned from Frank to Straeger, confused.

"Rest your weary brain, Todd," Straeger said. He took a pipe off the desk and then sat in an armchair in the corner. "Yes, MUX is alive and well, thank you, and I am pleased to be a member of its espionage department—an organization that could give *you* a few pointers, I'm afraid to say."

"Don't tell me this whole place is a front for MUX," Frank said.

Straeger laughed. "Nothing quite so grand. Only my little organization, Straeger Security, is involved."

"And who's *your* boss, Straeger?" Frank pressed. "What's his name, or don't you underlings know?"

"I believe we're ahead of ourselves," Straeger said, dismissing the question. He gestured toward his assistant, the short man with slicked-back dark hair. "Proper introductions have not been made. This is my right-hand man, Mr. Ciejki. He and a few others, including Mr. Brewster and Mr. Muldoon, make up my entire staff. Several months ago there was a series of break-ins that left the center's previous security staff completely baffled. When they decided to hire another firm, I applied."

"You also just *happened* to figure out how those break-ins occurred," Frank said, "because you staged them."

"I'm impressed. There may be a job for you here—depending on what we decide to do with you." Straeger smiled and began pacing the room. "My job has given me the opportunity to hear about many fascinating new technologies—including the wonderful new development called Battlechip at Prometheus."

Straeger stopped his pacing and snapped

around to face Frank eye to eye. "With the bonus I make for delivering Battlechip to MUX, I'll be able to retire. When you reach my age you'll understand how important that is."

With that he grabbed the phone off his desk and dialed a number. Lifting the receiver to his face, he frowned at the drumlike mechanical device attached to the mouthpiece. "I detest this thing." He stopped grumbling abruptly and smiled. "Greetings, Mr. Hardy. . . . No, we haven't spoken. Does my voice sound familiar?" He laughed.

"Well, I know you're struggling with an important decision," Straeger continued, "but I'm happy to say I have a proposition that will make it easier for you to decide. You see, we now have your wife *and* your son, Frank, who is quite a clever boy. We've given you plenty of time. . . . What's that? . . . Exactly as we discussed. . . . Yes, very good. . . . Oh, that won't be necessary, Mr. Hardy. Thank you and goodbye."

Frank didn't like the self-satisfied smile on Straeger's face. "What did he say?" he asked.

Straeger took a drag from his pipe. "'I will unlock doors to let your men in, if I have to. Just don't hurt my family.'"

"You're bluffing!" Frank shot back.

Straeger raised an eyebrow. "I am? Perhaps

you'd like me to call back so you can speak to him yourself."

Frank turned away. He knew Straeger was telling the truth. Humiliation washed over him. He had gone to Marfield to help out and ended up forcing his dad's hand.

"Now only one problem remains," Straeger said, drumming his fingers on the desk. "Where shall we keep this young firebrand?"

Brewster smiled. "I could give him a job."

"We can't let him wander around here," Ciejki said. "He'll blow our cover."

"I think the only safe place is right here in my inner office," Straeger said. "Mr. Brewster, I leave him in your capable hands. When I have obtained Battlechip I'll tell you to let him go."

"Right," Brewster said with a snicker.

"Why don't I believe you?" Frank asked.

"Do I detect a note of distrust in your question?" Straeger replied. He laughed. "Not to worry, Mr. Hardy. I always keep my promises. I've found it's the best way to insure that people will believe my threats."

"I'm impressed," Frank said dully.

Straeger turned toward the door. "Well, now, if you'll excuse me, gentlemen, I'm off to Bayport. Mr. Ciejki will take my place while I'm gone."

He opened the door for Ciejki, then gave one last wave as he stepped into the hallway.

Alone with Frank, Brewster reached into a desk drawer and pulled out a pair of handcuffs. He opened them and stuck the keys into his back pocket. "Okay, wise guy," he said, "sit down—now!"

Two hours later Frank was still in the office in a chair, his ankle cuffed to the desk leg, which was bolted to the floor. He had looked at all twelve pictures on the desk calendar, leafed through the desktop dictionary, and solved the crossword puzzle in the newspaper. He was drowning in boredom.

For what seemed like the thousandth time Frank scanned the room. A couple of feet behind him was a wall unit that contained a few notebooks, statuettes, glass figurines, and other knickknacks.

This time an idea hit him.

He looked across the desk. Brewster was sitting there, staring at the sports page of the Marfield *Sentinel*. He was fighting to keep his eyes open. His head fell to his chest, then jolted up when he realized he was falling asleep.

Frank opened his mouth into a wide yawn. He stretched his arms up, rocking back on his chair. His fingertips extended to the wall unit, and he felt the cold, smooth surface of a glass figurine. He closed his hand around it as Brewster's head began to sag again.

With a sudden sweep of his arm Frank brought the statue down on Brewster's head.

"Wha—" was the guard's last utterance before he slid off his chair and lay crumpled on the floor.

Frank stood up and pivoted on his bound ankle. Supporting himself on his free leg, he leaned toward the body. He was able to reach into Brewster's back pocket for the handcuff keys and unlock himself.

Shaking out his legs, Frank dropped the keys on the floor near Brewster. "Sorry I was such dull company," he said.

With that he sprinted for the window, lifted it, and had one foot out when he felt a tug on the right leg as Brewster's hand closed around his ankle.

# Chapter

# 15

FRANK KICKED BACK, his heel catching Brewster on the jaw. It was a soft blow but enough to finish the guard, who was really out this time. Frank sprinted for the center's exit.

After retrieving the Firebird and phoning his dad to say he had escaped, Frank drove straight to Prometheus.

"Mr. Hardy! I've been expecting you! Where have you been?" Mr. Winthrop greeted him.

"I was tied up for a while," Frank answered with a straight face.

The head of security was wearing a belted windbreaker and a pair of sun goggles as he greeted Frank at the gate to Prometheus

Computing. He waved Frank into courtyard B.

Surprised by the friendly greeting, Frank drove in with Mr. Winthrop trotting behind him. In the same spot where he and Joe had been ambushed the day before a helicopter was waiting.

"What a difference from last time!" Frank said, stepping out of the Firebird.

Mr. Winthrop smiled. "This time we are working together." He signaled the pilot to start the engine, then directed Frank around to the passenger side. "Your father just called a couple of minutes ago to say I should expect you. He told me all the details. Apparently your brother and a friend did a little reconnaissance work, and they think they found the kidnappers' hiding place."

"Is it a boat in Bayport Harbor?" Frank shouted after he climbed in.

"Exactly," Mr. Winthrop shouted back to be heard over the roar of the turning rotors. "How did you know?"

"I've done a little reconnaissance of my own," Frank said loudly.

Mr. Winthrop nodded, then gestured toward the helicopter pilot. "Edward's a top-notch pilot; you're in good hands. Your father will be waiting for you when you arrive in Bayport.

He's on the kidnappers' tail and may have located them by then."

"You mean Dad *didn't* arrange for a break-in at Prometheus after all?" Frank asked with cautious optimism.

Mr. Winthrop laughed. "You certainly have had your ears open, haven't you? Yes, he just called a few minutes ago to arrange for a break-in—with our full knowledge and help. My men and your father's special SWAT team will be waiting to give the intruders a very rude surprise!"

"All ri-i-ight!" Frank exclaimed, pulling the door shut. Rising slowly into the skies above Prometheus, he let out a whoop. Now if only his mom were okay . . . but he had to trust Joe and his dad to help her.

The helicopter covered the distance between Marfield and Bayport in a little over two hours. Fenton Hardy was waiting for them at a weed-strewn parking lot next to an abandoned train yard.

As they descended Frank looked at his watch, which now read two-thirty. He hoped they weren't too late. If Straeger had gotten there and found out Mr. Hardy wasn't home . . .

When the helicopter touched down Mr. Hardy opened Frank's door. "Am I glad to see you all in one piece!" He gave Edward a friendly wave. "Come on," he urged as Frank climbed out. "We don't have any time to lose—they have Joe now, too! There's a boat waiting for us at the harbor!"

"I didn't tell you when I called, but Straeger works undercover for MUX at the Center for Experimental Research," Frank said.

Fenton Hardy cocked an eyebrow. "Good old MUX again, huh? Nice work, Frank—let's finish up!"

The two Hardys ran toward a rented van at the edge of the lot and climbed in.

In minutes they pulled up beside a slip on the Bayport waterfront. An ancient fishing boat bobbed in the water. In front of it Captain Claes stood waiting.

"Thanks for the use of your boat, Claes!" Mr. Hardy called out. "I don't know how I can repay you."

There was a sly glint in the captain's eyes. "Give me time. I'll think of something."

Mr. Hardy, carrying a loaded revolver in a holster, boarded the old boat first. Frank followed, stepping around the air tanks and masks that lay on the floor of the boat.

On Mr. Hardy's fourth tug at the engine cord, the outboard motor finally caught. The boat putted out into the harbor.

"At this rate we'll be there by nightfall," Frank remarked.

"It's the best the old tub can do," Mr. Hardy replied. "They'll be on the lookout for something a little more sophisticated. The element of surprise will be on our side. Give me a hand," Fenton Hardy said, grabbing a fishing net. Frank helped him hook it over the side of the boat. "We have to look authentic."

"Right," Frank replied. "And anything we catch will be our dinner tonight."

Before long an abandoned sailboat came into view. "That must be Joe's," Mr. Hardy said. "Let's anchor here."

Frank threw out the anchor, then joined his dad and put on an air tank. Mr. Hardy sealed his gun in a watertight plastic pouch. Masks in place, they fell backward into the harbor and began swimming underwater.

Frank was the first to find the anchor cable. He climbed up, peeked into the yacht to see the secluded section of the deck behind the wheelhouse, then signaled his father to come aboard.

They huddled silently and listened to an agitated voice from inside the wheelhouse.

"*Iron Maiden*, Matyus calling. . . . Yes, I read you. . . . It *what?* Speak slower. . . . No. Who was caught? . . . I'll report it to Straeger immediately!"

They heard Matyus hang up the phone. Then his voice took on a hollow sound as he spoke into an intercom. "Mr. Straeger, that was Marfield—"

"Marvelous, Matyus," Straeger replied. "I can finally release these Hardys."

"Uh, well, not exactly, sir," Matyus said. "Frank Hardy has already escaped, and the raid on Prometheus has been turned back."

"What do you mean, 'has been turned back?'" Straeger asked, not concerning himself with Frank's escape.

"It seems that the raid has been ambushed, sir," Matyus said, his voice a little shaky. "Apparently it was all a setup—"

*"Whaaat?"*

"Most of the men were captured, including Todd Brewster, but two did escape."

"That's impossible! Fenton Hardy gave me his word the doors would be open and no one would interfere. He wouldn't have been foolish enough to pull something like this!"

"Would you like me to give you the details, sir?"

There was a long silence. Frank stole a glance at his dad, who nodded at him and gave him a confident wink.

"No, Captain Matyus." Straeger's voice, sounding sinister and tinny, came over the intercom system. "Set a course for the open sea. I would like you to join me down here in the engine room. At the moment I feel no bitterness or anger, only sadness.''

"Sadness, sir?"

"Yes. It has turned out to be a very sad day—for Mrs. Hardy and her son Joe!"

# Chapter

## 16

FRANK FELT BLOOD rise to his face. There was no time to lose. He turned to his father.

"Dad, I—"

But his father wasn't there. Frank crept to the stairway and looked down, then he peered around the wheelhouse cabin.

No Fenton Hardy.

Was he hiding, or had he raced down the stairs?

A sudden thought made him stay where he was. If his dad had wanted him along, he would have said so. Hadn't he jumped out of the van without explanation in the Springfield traffic the day before, only to return with the rented car that had saved them?

Chances were that something was up his father's sleeve now, too.

"Stop gawking and pull up anchor, Farrell!" Captain Matyus's voice barked to another man. "Steer this tank out into the Atlantic, top speed. I'm going down to join Straeger."

Frank heard the wheelhouse door squeak open, then slam shut. He ducked around the cabin, taking care to stay low. Captain Matyus circled the other side and descended the stairs.

When the captain had disappeared Frank craned his neck to look into the wheelhouse above him. He could see only one person moving around.

Suddenly there was a loud groan inches from him. Frank jumped, his heart beating wildly.

He looked around to see a mechanized pulley slowly turning, pulling the anchor cable out of the water.

With a soft *fooom* the yacht's engines purred to life.

They were on their way—out to the open Atlantic, where getaways were cleaner, where bodies could be disposed of and never found.

Frank knew exactly what he had to do now. He slipped around to the wheelhouse door. This Farrell was alone inside, gripping the steering wheel. Frank pulled the door open. A gust of air rushing in blew two sheets off a stack of papers inside.

Farrell let out a sigh of frustration. He bent down to scoop the papers off the floor, his back still to Frank. Frank edged forward.

Stuffing the papers in his trouser pocket, Farrell returned to the wheel. As the boat turned a flash of sun shone through a window and glinted against the chrome on the wheel's housing.

Frank was now three feet from him—two—Farrell stood stock-still, concentrating on his work.

Frank took a karate stance, poised for attack. He would make a statement, and when Farrell turned, he would—

*Thwock.*

"Oof!"

Frank felt a sharp pain in his gut. His breath whooshed out of his mouth as if he were a burst balloon. Stumbling backward, his arms flailing, he barely saw Farrell retract the backward kick he had just uncorked.

"Like to attack from behind, eh?" Farrell gloated. "You should check there aren't any mirrors first!"

Of course! Frank realized. The chrome. He was watching my reflection in the chrome.

He scrambled to his feet—but not before Farrell took a roundhouse swing with his right fist. Frank jerked his head back but caught part of the blow on his jaw. He staggered into the side of a table.

Gripping the table, he yanked it back.

It wouldn't budge.

"Sorry, pal, it's attached," Farrell said, sending another punch to Frank's stomach.

Frank let his reflexes do the thinking. His left arm shot out and blocked the punch. Planting a foot, he let fly a kick that connected with Farrell's chest.

Farrell spun around and snatched a fire extinguisher off the wall next to the door. He pivoted, pointing the nozzle at Frank.

"Pretty wimpy weapon, if you ask me," Frank said.

"Who asked you?" Farrell replied. He squeezed the trigger, sending a jet stream of white chemical spray toward Frank.

Frank turned and dropped to the floor. The chemical soaked the area around him. He jumped to his feet and ran to the ship's controls. With a flick of the gearshift he put the engine in neutral. To the right of the shift was a switch labeled "Anchor." He turned it from "Up" to "Down." There was an abrupt grinding noise, then a hum as the anchor lowered itself. For now, the *Iron Maiden* wasn't going anywhere.

"Hey!" Farrell shouted, and he lost his footing on the cabin floor, slick with white foam. He fell with his feet in the air.

"Well, one good turn deserves another," Frank said. As Farrell scrambled to his feet Frank connected with an uppercut to the sailor's jaw.

Farrell flew against the wall and sank to the floor. The fire extinguisher hit the floor with a loud clank.

Frank braced himself, but Farrell was motionless. He stepped back toward the ship-to-shore phone and snatched the receiver off the hook.

"Operator," a faint voice said.

Farrell's chest heaved calmly up and down. Frank unclenched his fists when he realized his adversary was unconscious.

"Operator," the voice repeated.

"Uh, yes," Frank spoke into the receiver. "I'd like the Bayport—"

Just then a menacing voice filled the room, and Frank fell silent.

# Chapter

## 17

"OUCH!" JOE WINCED as a bobby pin snapped in the lock and dug into his finger.

"Did you get it?" Mrs. Hardy asked.

"No, it got me," Joe replied. "I don't think this is going to work." He eyed the metal table. "Maybe if we can pry this thing out of the floor and use it as a wedge—"

The hastening rhythm of footsteps moving toward them made him stop. Instinctively he glanced up at the phony stemware box. The lens of the hidden closed-circuit camera was still covered by the magazine he'd put up there.

He knew Matyus would find out about it sooner or later. Joe sat down and waited for his men to come in and rip down the magazine.

The door made a resounding clang as it

swung open and hit the metal wall. Captain Matyus glowered as he stormed in, but his expression was placid compared to that of the silver-haired man next to him.

It took Joe a moment to recognize who it was. "Hey, you're in on this thing, too, Straeger? I guess you're the stemware expert, huh?"

Immediately Joe wished he could swallow his words. Both men had pistols, and both were pointed straight at him.

Joe put his hands in the air and backed up. "Uh, sorry, fellas. Go ahead, take the magazines away. The camera's still in good shape; I didn't touch the lens."

Mrs. Hardy stood up and faced Straeger. "Who are you?"

"Mrs. Hardy, I hoped we would meet under happier circumstances," Straeger said, swinging the point of his gun to face her. "I had intended to come here as your liberator. I was prepared to have you escorted ashore with my apologies and a cheerful bon voyage. But clearly your husband regards your life—and your son's—with callous disrespect. He has failed to live up to his end of my simple bargain."

Joe stepped in front of his mother. "Put it down, Straeger. Before I came out here I notified people on shore, so it's only a matter of time before someone tracks you down. And you'd be better off with two prisoners than with two corpses.''

Straeger's eyes were blazing with a rage that was just this side of sanity. "Unlike your father, I am a man of principle. I always live up to my promises. Therefore I have no choice." He released the gun's safety and aimed carefully between Joe's eyes. "You have your father to blame for this, not me."

"Put it down, Straeger!"

Straeger and Matyus wheeled around. Joe felt his breath catch in his throat.

Standing in the door was Fenton Hardy, his gun pointed at Straeger.

"Well," Straeger said, a smile creeping across his face, "look what the sea washed up. Nice try, Mr. Hardy, but I believe one triumph per day is quite enough for you."

"I'm not so sure, Straeger," Mr. Hardy said. "You know, your little group is a thing of the past. Most of its members have been captured, and the ones that got away aren't likely to stick around waiting for their paychecks. So I'd suggest—"

"That Captain Matyus and I give ourselves up?" Straeger laughed. "Like son, like father. You think the whole thing has been neatly tied up, resolved, don't you? I have unfortunate news for you. At the moment Captain Matyus's first mate is setting a course for the open sea. This ship's shabby appearance camouflages one of the fastest yachts on the East Coast. In minutes we shall be miles from anyone foolish enough to try to give chase. And without the three of you on board we will only go faster."

"You forget, Straeger," Mr. Hardy said, "I'm armed."

Now it was Matyus's turn to laugh. "Yes, but you're also outnumbered, two guns to one."

Fenton Hardy nodded. "True. I am outnumbered. But one of the first things I learned as a detective was that it's not the bullets that count, but where they go."

Four sharp cracks rang through the room, four flashes of light. The bullets embedded themselves in the corner steampipe.

Geysers of hot steam exploded into the room. Joe and his mother spun around and crouched to the floor.

"Duck!" Captain Matyus yelled, pulling Straeger down.

"In the corner!" Fenton Hardy shouted to Joe.

Joe took his mother's hand and stepped back into the brig, away from the door, but she yanked free.

"No!" she said, her eyes focused on the spot where her husband was disappearing behind a cloud of steam. "He's going to burn to death!"

"Come on, Mom!" Joe insisted, dragging her into the corner of their jail.

He looked back, but the room was nothing but hot white vapor. Two shots rang out, accompanied by two sharp flashes of light.

"Fenton!" Mrs. Hardy shrieked.

There was a dull clatter. Joe tightened his grip on his mother's hand. He was having trouble seeing her now. He walked back toward the door, trying to wave a clear path through the steam.

"Get them!" came Captain Matyus's voice.

Just then Joe felt an iron grip on his forearm. He planted his feet and pushed against the unseen adversary.

"Joe, it's me!" He heard his father's whisper. "I blew the lock on the gate. Come on!"

Led by Mr. Hardy, the three of them blundered forward through the steam. Joe gritted his teeth against the searing heat. He knew that if they got *too* near the pipe . . .

"Get them," Straeger said, echoing Matyus. He was off to the Hardys' left. Fenton Hardy changed directions slightly and picked up the pace.

A moment later Joe felt the air temperature change. His skin began to cool.

They turned a corner, and the air began to

clear. Ahead of them stretched a corridor Joe hadn't seen.

"Where are we?" Joe asked.

"Haven't the foggiest," his father replied. "No pun intended."

All three of them spun around as Straeger loudly announced their escape on the intercom. Just then the *clonk* of heavy footsteps sounded on metal. "Down here!" an unfamiliar voice called out.

"They're coming out of the woodwork," Joe said. "They must have heard the shots."

They backed up and looked into a passageway on their left. Three more crew members, their faces grim and determined, were dropping through a hatch at the end of it.

"This way!" Joe said. He led them toward the right instead.

At the end of the hall Joe could make out a faint square outline of light on the ceiling. A small hatch. "We're out of here!" he shouted, sprinting toward the ladder that led to the hatch.

Joe scampered to the top and pushed against the hatch, once—twice—

It wouldn't budge.

"They're coming!" Mrs. Hardy said.

"Get down, Joe!" Mr. Hardy demanded. He pointed the pistol at the hatch.

Joe jumped down and stood back. Mr. Hardy took aim and fired.

*Click.* The sound was small and pathetic.

Fenton Hardy's eyes widened. "I shot the full round in the brig," he said in disbelief.

Joe climbed up the ladder again and rammed his shoulder against it. A jolt of pain shot through him, and the hatch stayed put.

"Is there another path?" Mrs. Hardy asked.

"The only thing we can do is backtrack—"

"There they are!" a voice echoed into their passageway.

Joe stood frozen on the ladder. On either side of him were his mother and father. He squeezed their hands and felt his throat turn to cotton as a battalion of six armed men charged toward them.

And he felt himself go numb as Straeger's voice pierced the humid air: "Shoot to kill!"

# Chapter

# 18

IN A BURST OF ENERGY, Joe tried the hatch one more time. There was a dull thud and a cracking sound.

I'm breaking it, Joe thought. Just one more shove.

*"Get down!"* Mrs. Hardy cried. *"They're shooting at you!"*

So that's what the crack was. Joe fell to the floor. A bullet whizzed just over his head.

Suddenly Straeger's voice could be heard again: "Cease fire!"

The passageway fell silent except for a faint murmuring among the crew members. They stepped aside as Straeger pushed his way through to the front.

He stood in the dimly lit corridor facing the Hardy family, his gun ready at his side.

"I want to see this," he said. "I want the pleasure of returning the humiliation I've received at your hands, Mr. Hardy. How does it feel to have your life's plan thwarted? How does it feel to stand in front of a firing squad and know your family is to be shot in seconds?"

"I thought you said we were moving out to sea!" Joe blurted out.

"Don't try to distract me," Straeger shot back.

"I didn't feel us accelerate," Joe continued.

"The engine is quite silent," Straeger said.

"Sure feels like it's idling to me."

"Ready . . ." Straeger called out.

The crew members lifted their weapons.

"Don't you think this is overkill?" Joe tried in desperation.

Above him there was a sudden clomping noise on the deck.

"Aim . . ."

The clomping turned into a knocking. A shaft of light slanted down into the corridor from the ceiling above.

"What the—" Straeger muttered.

Joe looked up. The hatch was moving!

Captain Matyus appeared behind Straeger.

"Hold it!" he ordered. "Farrell, if that's you up there, knock it off, or you'll be shot, too!"

"Farrell, eh?" came a muffled voice from outside the hatch. "Close—both are two syllables and Irish. But you don't get a cigar, my friend!"

Joe couldn't believe what he was hearing. When the hatch flew open his disbelief flew out.

A familiar, beefy man in a blue uniform stared down at them, his hand clutching a revolver. *"Riley*'s the name. Officer Con Riley, Bayport Police. Hands up, everyone, and drop those weapons. You're surrounded."

"Hi, Mom. Everything all right?" Frank smiled pleasantly over Riley's shoulder. "Seems a little warm down there."

"Frank!" Mrs. Hardy said, enjoying the sound of the name as if she were saying it for the first time.

Joe felt an unexpected laugh erupt. "Yeah, it's hot down here, all right. In fact, I think it's time we put old Straeger here on ice."

"With pleasure," Officer Riley said with a smile. Then his voice became a drill sergeant's bark. "All right, everybody out here—on the double. And don't try anything funny. I've got the entire Bayport Harbor Police with me!"

Straeger's face broke into a cheerful, slightly baffled smile. He handed his gun to one of the

143

sailors. "Officer Riley, I must say I'm happy to see you, but I think you've been misled. It is *we* who require your services. These people are trespassing on our ship."

"I see," said Riley. "You just happened to be anchored way out here, playing idly with all this fancy equipment, when Fenton, Laura, and their sons decided to break in."

"I can't speak for them, officer, but Mr. Hardy did shoot holes in the ship's pipes. Steam is billowing through every hallway down here."

"Straeger, I believe you like I believe in the tooth fairy," Riley remarked.

Straeger laughed. "Well, then you may end up with a quarter under your pillow. With all due respect, I don't think you can arrest us if the evidence is in our favor."

Riley looked from Straeger to Mr. Hardy and shrugged. "I suppose you're right about that. And it follows you have nothing to hide." Then he shouted over his shoulder: "Wyman, Hastings! Come with me. The rest of you guard the deck and make sure no one leaves."

By this time Matyus and most of the yacht's crew had been herded upstairs and onto the deck. Officer Riley and two other police officers climbed down.

"You realize you won't be able to see a thing

in the engine room because of the steam,'' Straeger said.

"We'll just have to do our best," Riley replied.

"This way, gentlemen," Straeger said, ushering the three men past him. Mr. Hardy began to follow, but Straeger held out his arm. "I must request that Fenton Hardy stay behind. I see no reason that he should be with us."

Officer Riley sighed. "Fenton, wait here a minute, okay? I'll be right back."

"Make sure you check the engine room!" Joe called out.

As Riley walked down the companionway Joe heard Straeger say, "Of course, the engine room is off limits. Hot steam is spewing out, and you're likely to get burned."

"Don't you have someone fixing it yet?" Riley asked.

"Of course. But it will probably take hours."

As they disappeared into the steam at the end of the passageway Frank called down, "Mom, are you all right?"

"Fine," Mrs. Hardy said. "They gave me nautical magazines to read while I was in their little jail. When we get out of here I'll be able to build a boat."

"Don't get your hopes up," Joe said. "If

Officer Riley can't see the brig, he may have to let them go.''

"Come on, let's climb up," Mr. Hardy said. "At least we can wait in the fresh air."

Joe looked up to the open hatch. His brother was missing.

"Frank?" he called out.

One of the policemen gave a shrug and pointed to his right. "He ran off."

Joe climbed onto the deck, then helped his mother and father out. The afternoon had become cool. Joe shivered slightly from the abrupt change in temperature.

"Where's Frank?" Mrs. Hardy asked.

A moment later they heard Frank's voice over a loudspeaker. "Attention, please—this includes you, Mr. Straeger. This is Frank Hardy with a message for Officer Riley. The steam-powered engines have been turned off. You may safely enter the engine room. Be sure to visit the cage of the escaped prisoners on your left and see the marvelous hidden-camera-in-the-stemware-box trick!"

Joe, Mr. Hardy, and Mrs. Hardy ran into the wheelhouse. Frank greeted them with a smile. "Well, I give them about—oh, fifteen minutes!"

"Long enough for a little family time," Fenton Hardy said. "A little story-swapping about the last few days. What do you say we sit on the deck?'' He put one arm around Frank and the other around his wife.

"I'm not sure I want three rubber wet suits next to me,'' said Laura Hardy, taking in the three men in her family all dressed in identical black rubber.

"So who aw na yur?'' Chet Morton mumbled, his mouth stuffed full of Aunt Gertrude's Swedish meatballs.

Mr. Hardy cast a puzzled glance around the dining room table. "Would someone like to translate?''

"I think he said, 'Who's on your—something,' '' Tony Prito tried.

"Talk, talk, talk,'' Aunt Gertrude said, shaking her head as she heated up a new batch of tomato sauce on the stove. "You're all talking a mile a minute about this awful adventure, and I can't understand a word of it! *Swallow* first!''

"Owned the *yacht,*'' Chet said, wiping his mouth with a napkin. "Who owned the yacht? Did the police find out?''

"Uh-huh,'' Joe replied, quickly swallowing his food. "It's registered under the name Matyus Shipping, which turns out to be a subsidiary of MUX.''

"So by capturing Matyus and Straeger we've managed to smash two important MUX espionage rings,'' Frank went on.

"What happens next?" Biff Hooper piped up. "Does the whole organization come tumbling down?"

Fenton Hardy exhaled. "Unfortunately, no. We wouldn't have even known Matyus and Straeger were connected if we hadn't found them together on that yacht. In fact, I believe they hadn't even known each other until this caper."

Laura Hardy looked puzzled. "Then who introduced them?"

"That's the big question," Mr. Hardy answered. "There's somebody at the top, somebody we've never been able to come close to. He's covered himself with layers and layers of umbrella organizations."

"Straeger and Matyus both claim they don't know his name," Joe said. "They just accept his orders through anonymous couriers."

"It makes me shudder to think there may be more of those ruthless men out there somewhere," Aunt Gertrude said.

"Oh, we'll track them down," Frank said. He was speaking to Aunt Gertrude, but his eyes were looking into the distance. "As long as there's an MUX, we'll be right behind them."

A silence settled over the room, interrupted only by the clicking of forks on the plates.

"By the way," Mr. Hardy said, "tomorrow

the Marfield police are auctioning all the stuff they found in Straeger's office. Anybody want to go?''

Phil Cohen's eyes lit up. "Any electronic equipment?"

"You bet," Mr. Hardy said. "A fax machine, a copier, an answering machine, a couple of printers, and—something else."

"Mmb awuhnuhk!" Chet blurted out, his mouth full again.

Mr. Hardy snapped his fingers. "That's what it was. The voice scrambler!"

As the table broke into laughter Chet Morton's face slowly turned the color of Aunt Gertrude's tomato sauce.

## Frank and Joe's next case:

The Hardys and friend Callie Shaw are off to Washington, D.C. Callie finally has the chance to meet her Parisian pen pal, Madeleine Berot, whose parents have been assigned to the French embassy. But when Maddy is caught shoplifting, Frank and Joe suspect that there's something rotten in the state of French diplomacy.

Determined to get to the bottom of the Madeleine Berot mystery, the Hardys find themselves caught in a web of international intrigue. They take off on a tingling chase through the nation's capital, pursuing a gang of continental con artists. In a case of D.C. deceit, it's up to Frank and Joe to nip the caper in the bud . . . in *Diplomatic Deceit*, Case #38 in The Hardy Boys Casefiles™.